THE GREAT STONE OF SARDIS

FRANK R. STOCKTON

1ˢᵗ WORLD
LIBRARY
Literary Society

The Great Stone of Sardis

Frank R. Stockton

© 1st World Library, 2007
PO Box 2211
Fairfield, IA 52556
www.1stworldlibrary.com
First Edition

LCCN: 2007927771

Softcover ISBN: 978-1-4218-4539-5
Hardcover ISBN: 978-1-4218-4455-8
eBook ISBN: 978-1-4218-4623-1

Purchase *"The Great Stone of Sardis"*
as a traditional bound book at:
www.1stWorldLibrary.com/purchase.asp?ISBN=978-1-4218-4539-5

1st World Library is a literary, educational organization
dedicated to:

- Creating a free internet library of downloadable ebooks

- Hosting writing competitions and offering book publishing scholarships.

Interested in more 1st World Library books? contact:
literacy@1stworldlibrary.com
Check us out at: www.1stworldlibrary.com

1st World Library Literary Society

Giving Back to the World

"If you want to work on the core problem, it's early school literacy."

- James Barksdale, former CEO of Netscape

"No skill is more crucial to the future of a child, or to a democratic and prosperous society, than literacy."

- Los Angeles Times

"Literacy... means far more than learning how to read and write... The aim is to transmit... knowledge and promote social participation."

- UNESCO

"Literacy is not a luxury, it is a right and a responsibility. If our world is to meet the challenges of the twenty-first century we must harness the energy and creativity of all our citizens."

- President Bill Clinton

"Parents should be encouraged to read to their children, and teachers should be equipped with all available techniques for teaching literacy, so the varying needs and capacities of individual kids can be taken into account."

- Hugh Mackay

CONTENTS

CHAPTER I

THE ARRIVAL OF THE EUTERPE-THALIA

It was about noon of a day in early summer that a westward-bound Atlantic liner was rapidly nearing the port of New York. Not long before, the old light-house on Montauk Point had been sighted, and the company on board the vessel were animated by the knowledge that in a few hours they would be at the end of their voyage.

The vessel now speeding along the southern coast of Long Island was the Euterpe-Thalia, from Southampton. On Wednesday morning she had left her English port, and many of her passengers were naturally anxious to be on shore in time to transact their business on the last day of the week. There were even some who expected to make their return voyage on the Melpomene-Thalia, which would leave New York on the next Monday.

The Euterpe-Thalia was one of those combination ocean vessels which had now been in use for nearly ten years, and although the present voyage was not a particularly rapid one, it had been made in a little less than three days.

As may be easily imagined, a vessel like this was a very different craft from the old steamers which used to cross the

Atlantic—"ocean greyhounds" they were called—in the latter part of the nineteenth century.

It would be out of place here to give a full description of the vessels which at the period of our story, in 1947, crossed the Atlantic at an average time of three days, but an idea of their construction will suffice. Most of these vessels belonged to the class of the Euterpe-Thalia, and were, in fact, compound marine structures, the two portions being entirely distinct from each other. The great hull of each of these vessels contained nothing but its electric engines and its propelling machinery, with the necessary fuel and adjuncts.

The upper portion of the compound vessel consisted of decks and quarters for passengers and crew and holds for freight. These were all comprised within a vast upper hull, which rested upon the lower hull containing the motive power, the only point of contact being an enormous ball-and-socket joint. Thus, no matter how much the lower hull might roll and pitch and toss, the upper hull remained level and comparatively undisturbed.

Not only were comfort to passengers and security to movable freight gained by this arrangement of the compound vessel, but it was now possible to build the lower hull of much less size than had been the custom in the former days of steamships, when the hull had to be large enough to contain everything. As the more modern hull held nothing but the machinery, it was small in comparison with the super-incumbent upper hull, and thus the force of the engine, once needed to propel a vast mass through the resisting medium of the ocean, was now employed upon a comparatively small hull, the great body of the vessel meeting with no resistance except that of the air.

It was not necessary that the two parts of these compound vessels should always be the same. The upper hulls belonging to one of the transatlantic lines were generally so constructed that they could be adjusted to any one of their lower or motive-power hulls. Each hull had a name of its own, and so the combination name of the entire vessel was frequently changed.

It was not three o'clock when the Euterpe-Thalia passed through the Narrows and moved slowly towards her pier on the Long Island side of the city. The quarantine officers, who had accompanied the vessel on her voyage, had dropped their report in the official tug which had met the vessel on her entrance into the harbor, and as the old custom-house annoyances had long since been abolished, most of the passengers were prepared for a speedy landing.

One of these passengers—a man about thirty-five—stood looking out over the stern of the vessel instead of gazing, as were most of his companions, towards the city which they were approaching. He looked out over the harbor, under the great bridge gently spanning the distance between the western end of Long Island and the New Jersey shore—its central pier resting where once lay the old Battery—and so he gazed over the river, and over the houses stretching far to the west, as if his eyes could catch some signs of the country far beyond. This was Roland Clewe, the hero of our story, who had been studying and experimenting for the past year in the scientific schools and workshops of Germany. It was towards his own laboratory and his own workshops, which lay out in the country far beyond the wide line of buildings and settlements which line the western bank of the Hudson, that his heart went out and his eyes vainly strove to follow.

Skilfully steered, the Thalia moved slowly between high stone piers of massive construction; but the Euterpe, or upper part of the vessel, did not pass between the piers, but over them both, and when the pier-heads projected beyond her stern the motion of the lower vessel ceased; then the great piston, which supported the socket in which the ball of the Euterpe moved, slowly began to descend into the central portion of the Thalia, and as the tide was low, it was not long before each side of the upper hull rested firmly and securely upon the stone piers. Then the socket on the lower vessel descended rapidly until it was entirely clear of the ball, and the Thalia backed out from between the piers to take its place in a dock where it would be fitted for the voyage of the next day but one, when it would move under the Melpomene, resting on its piers a short distance below, and, adjusting its socket to her ball, would lift her free from the piers and carry her across the ocean.

The pier of the Euterpe was not far from the great Long Island and New Jersey Bridge, and Roland Clewe, when he reached the broad sidewalk which ran along the river-front, walked rapidly towards the bridge. When he came to it he stepped into one of the elevators, which were placed at intervals along its sides from the waterfront to the far-distant point where it touched the land, and in company with a dozen other pedestrians speedily rose to the top of the bridge, on which moved two great platforms or floors, one always keeping on its way to the east, and the other to the west. The floor of the elevator detached itself from the rest of the structure and kept company with the movable platform until all of its passengers had stepped on to the latter, when it returned with such persons as wished to descend at that point.

As Clewe took his way along the platform, walking westward with it, as if he would thus hasten his arrival at the other end of the bridge, he noticed that great improvements had been made during his year of absence. The structures on the platforms, to which people might retire in bad weather or when they wished refreshments, were more numerous and apparently better appointed than when he had seen them last, and the long rows of benches on which passengers might sit in the open air during their transit had also increased in number. Many people walked across the bridge, taking their exercise, while some who were out for the air and the sake of the view walked in the direction opposite to that in which the platform was moving, thus lengthening the pleasant trip.

At the great elevator over the old Battery many passengers went down and many came up, but the wide platforms still moved to the east and moved to the west, never stopping or changing their rate of speed.

Roland Clewe remained on the bridge until he had reached its western end, far out on the old Jersey flats, and there he took a car of the suspended electric line, which would carry him to his home, some fifty miles in the interior. The rails of this line ran along the top of parallel timbers, some twenty feet from the ground, and below and between these rails the cars were suspended, the wheels which rested on the rails being attached near the top of the car. Thus it was impossible for the cars to run off the track; and as their bottoms or floors were ten or twelve feet from the ground, they could meet with no dangerous obstacles. In consequence of the safety of this structure, the trains were run at a very high speed.

Roland Clewe was a man who had given his life, even before he ceased to be a boy, to the investigation of physical science and its applications, and those who thought they knew him called him a great inventor; but he, who knew himself better than any one else could know him, was aware that, so far, he had not invented anything worthy the power which he felt within himself.

After the tidal wave of improvements and discoveries which had burst upon the world at the end of the nineteenth century there had been a gradual subsidence of the waters of human progress, and year by year they sank lower and lower, until, when the twentieth century was yet young, it was a common thing to say that the human race seemed to have gone backward fifty or even a hundred years.

It had become fashionable to be unprogressive. Like old furniture in the century which had gone out, old manners, customs, and ideas had now become more attractive than those which were modern and present. Philosophers said that society was retrograding, that it was becoming satisfied with less than was its due; but society answered that it was falling back upon the things of its ancestors, which were sounder and firmer, more simple and beautiful, more worthy of the true man and woman, than all that mass of harassing improvement which had swept down upon mankind in the troubled and nervous days at the end of the nineteenth century.

On the great highways, smooth and beautiful, the stage-coach had taken the place to a great degree of the railroad train; the steamship, which moved most evenly and with less of the jarring and shaking consequent upon high speed, was the favored vessel with ocean travellers. It was not considered good form to read the daily papers; and only those hurried to their business who were obliged to do so in order that their employers might attend to their affairs in the leisurely manner which was then the custom of the business world.

Fast horses had become almost unknown, and with those who still used these animals a steady walker was the favorite. Bicycles had gone out as the new century came in, it being a matter of course that they should be superseded by the new electric vehicles of every sort and fashion, on which one could work the pedals if he desired exercise, or sit quietly if his inclinations were otherwise, and only the very young or the intemperate allowed themselves rapid motion on their electric wheels. It would have been considered as vulgar at that time to speed over a smooth road as it would have been

Frank R. Stockton

thought in the nineteenth century to run along the city sidewalk.

People thought the world moved slower; at all events, they hoped it would soon do so. Even the wiser revolutionists postponed their outbreaks. Success, they believed, was fain to smile upon effort which had been well postponed.

Men came to look upon a telegram as an insult; the telephone was preferred, because it allowed one to speak slowly if he chose. Snap-shot cameras were found only in the garrets. The fifteen minutes' sittings now in vogue threw upon the plate the color of the eyes, hair, and the flesh tones of the sitter. Ladies wore hoop skirts.

But these days of passivism at last passed by; earnest thinkers had not believed in them; they knew they were simply reactionary, and could not last; and the century was not twenty years old when the world found itself in a storm of active effort never known in its history before. Religion, politics, literature, and art were called upon to get up and shake themselves free of the drowsiness of their years of inaction.

On that great and crowded stage where the thinkers of the world were busy in creating new parts for themselves without much reference to what other people were doing in their parts, Roland Clewe was now ready to start again, with more earnestness and enthusiasm than before, to essay a character which, if acted as he wished to act it, would give him exceptional honor and fame, and to the world, perhaps, exceptional advantage.

CHAPTER II

THE SARDIS WORKS

At the little station of Sardis, in the hill country of New Jersey, Roland Clewe alighted from the train, and almost instantly his hand was grasped by an elderly man, plainly and even roughly dressed, who appeared wonderfully glad to see him. Clewe also was greatly pleased at the meeting.

"Tell me, Samuel, how goes everything?" said Clewe, as they walked off. "Have you anything to say that you did not telegraph? How is your wife?"

"She's all right," was the answer. "And there's nothin' happened, except, night before last, a man tried to look into your lens-house."

"How did he do that?" exclaimed Clewe, suddenly turning upon his companion. "I am amazed! Did he use a ladder?"

Old Samuel grinned. "He couldn't do that, you know, for the flexible fence would keep him off. No; he sailed over the place in one of those air-screw machines, with a fan workin' under the car to keep it up."

"And so he soared up above my glass roof and looked down, I suppose?"

Frank R. Stockton

"That's what he did," said Samuel; "but he had a good deal of trouble doin' it. It was moonlight, and I watched him."

"Why didn't you fire at him?" asked Clewe. "Or at least let fly one of the ammonia squirts and bring him down?"

"I wanted to see what he would do," said the old man. "The machine he had couldn't be steered, of course. He could go up well enough, but the wind took him where it wanted to. But I must give this feller the credit of sayin' that he managed his basket pretty well. He carried it a good way to the windward of the lens-house, and then sent it up, expectin' the wind to take it directly over the glass roof, but it shifted a little, and so he missed the roof and had to try it again. He made two or three bad jobs of it, but finally managed it by hitchin' a long cord to a tree, and then the wind held him there steady enough to let him look down for a good while."

"You don't tell me that!" cried Clewe. "Did you stay there and let him look down into my lens-house?"

The old man laughed. "I let him look down," said he, "but he didn't see nothin'. I was laughin' at him all the time he was at work. He had his instruments with him, and he was turnin' down his different kinds of lights, thinkin', of course, that he could see through any kind of coverin' that we put over our machines; but, bless you! he couldn't do nothin', and I could almost hear him swear as he rubbed his eyes after he had been lookin' down for a little while."

Clewe laughed. "I see," said he. "I suppose you turned on the photo-hose."

"That's just what I did," said the old man. "Every night while you were away I had the lens-room filled with the revolving-light squirts, and when these were turned on I knew there was no gettin' any kind of rays through them. A feller may look through a roof and a wall, but he can't look through light comin' the other way, especially when it's twistin' and curlin' and spittin'."

"That's a capital idea," said Clewe. "I never thought of using the photo-hose in that way. But there are very few people in this world who would know anything about my new lens machinery even if they saw it. This fellow must have been that Pole, Rovinski. I met him in Europe, and I think he came over here not long before I did."

"That's the man, sir," said Samuel. "I turned a needle search-light on him just as he was givin' up the business, and I have got a little photograph of him at the house. His face is mostly beard, but you'll know him."

"What became of him?" asked Clewe.

"My light frightened him," he said, "and the wind took him over into the woods. I thought, as you were comin' home so soon, I wouldn't do nothin' more. You had better attend to him yourself."

"Very good," said Clewe. "I'll do that."

The home of Roland Clewe, a small house plainly furnished, but good enough for a bachelor's quarters, stood not half a mile from the station, and near it were the extensive buildings which he called his Works. Here were laboratories, large machine-shops in which many men were busy at all sorts of strange contrivances in metal and other materials; and besides other small edifices there was a great round tower-like structure, with smooth iron walls thirty feet high and without windows, and which was lighted and ventilated from the top. This was Clewe's special workshop; and besides old Samuel Block and such workmen as were absolutely necessary and could be trusted, few people ever entered it but himself. The industries in the various buildings were diverse, some of them having no apparent relation to the others. Each of them was expected to turn out something which would revolutionize something or other in this world, but it was to his lens-house that Roland Clewe gave, in these days, his special attention. Here a great enterprise was soon to begin, more important in his eyes than anything else which had engaged human endeavor.

When sometimes in his moments of reflection he felt obliged to consider the wonders of applied electricity, and give them their due place in comparison with the great problem he expected to solve, he had his moments of doubt. But these moments did not come frequently. The day would arrive when from his lens-house there would be promulgated a great discovery which would astonish the world.

During Roland Clewe's absence in Germany his works had been left under the general charge of Samuel Block. This old man was not a scientific person; he was not a skilled mechanic; in fact, he had been in early life a shoemaker. But when Roland Clewe, some five years before, had put up his works near the little village of Sardis, he had sent for Block, whom he had known all his life and who was at that time the tenant of a small farm, built a cottage for him and his wife, and told him to take care of the place. From planning the grounds and superintending fences, old Sammy had begun to keep an eye upon builders and mechanics; and, being a very shrewd man, he had gradually widened the sphere of his caretaking, until, at this time, he exercised a nominal supervision over all the buildings. He knew what was going on in each; he had a good idea, sometimes, of the scientific basis of this or that bit of machinery, and had gradually become acquainted with the workings and management of many of the instruments; and now and then he gave to his employer very good hints in regard to the means of attaining an end, more especially in the line of doing something by instrumentalities not intended for that purpose. If Sammy could take any machine which had been constructed to bore holes, and with it plug up orifices, he would consider that he had been of advantage to his kind.

Block was a thoroughly loyal man. The interests of his employer were always held by him first and above everything. But although the old man understood, sometimes very well, and always in a fair degree, what the inventor was trying to accomplish, and appreciated the magnitude and often the amazing nature of his operations, he never believed in any of them.

Sammy was a thoroughly old-fashioned man. He had been born and had grown up in the days when a steam-locomotive was good enough and fast enough for any sensible traveller, and he greatly preferred a good pair of horses to any vehicle which one steered with a handle and regulated the speed thereof with a knob. Roland Clew e might devise all the wonderful contrivances he pleased, and he might do all sorts of astonishing things with them, but Sammy would still be of the opinion that, even if the machines did all that they were expected to do, the things they did generally would not be worth the doing.

Still, the old man would not interfere by word or deed with any of the plans or actions of his employer. On the contrary, he would help him in every possible way—by fidelity, by suggestion, by constant devotion and industry; but, in spite of all that, it was one of the most firmly founded principles of his life that Roland Clewe had no right to ask him to believe in the value of the wild and amazing schemes he had on hand.

Before Roland Clewe slept that night he had visited all his workshops, factories, and laboratories. His men had been busily occupied during his absence under the directions of their various special managers, and those in charge were of the opinion that everything had progressed as favorably and as rapidly as should have been expected; but Roland Clewe was not satisfied, even though many of his inventions and machines were much nearer completion than he had expected to find them. The work necessary to be done in his lens-house before he could go on with the great work of his life was not yet finished.

As well as he could judge, it would be a month or two before he could devote himself to those labors in his lens-house the thought of which had so long filled his mind by day, and even during his sleep.

CHAPTER III

MARGARET RALEIGH

After breakfast the-following morning Roland Clewe mounted his horse and rode over to a handsome house which stood upon a hill about a mile and a half from Sardis. Horses, which had almost gone out of use during the first third of the century, were now getting to be somewhat in fashion again. Many people now appreciated the pleasure which these animals had given to the world since the beginning of history, and whose place, in an aesthetic sense, no inanimate machine could supply. As Roland Clewe swung himself from the saddle at the foot of a broad flight of steps, the house door was opened and a lady appeared.

"I saw you coming!" she exclaimed, running down the steps to meet him.

She was a handsome woman, inclined to be tall, and some five years younger than Clewe. This was Mrs. Margaret Raleigh, partner with Roland Clewe in the works at Sardis, and, in fact, the principal owner of that great estate. She was a widow, and her husband had been not only a man of science, but a very rich man; and when he died, at the outset of his career, his widow believed it her duty to devote his fortune to the prosecution and development of scientific works. She knew Roland Clewe as a hard student and worker, as a man of brilliant and original ideas, and as the originator of schemes which, if carried out successfully, would place him among the great inventors of the world.

She was not a scientific woman in the strict sense of the word, but she had a most thorough and appreciative sympathy with all forms of physical research, and there was a distinctiveness and grandeur in the aims towards which Roland Clewe had directed his life work which determined her to unite, with all the power of her money and her personal encouragement, in the labors he had set for himself.

Therefore it was that the main part of the fortune left by Herbert Raleigh had been invested in the shops and foundries at Sardis, and that Roland Clewe and Margaret Raleigh were partners and co-owners in the business and the plant of the establishment.

"I am glad to welcome you back," said she, her hand in his. "But it strikes me as odd to see you come upon a horse; I should have supposed that by this time you would arrive sliding over the tree-tops on a pair of aerial skates."

"No," said he. "I may invent that sort of thing, but I prefer to use a horse. Don't you remember my mare? I rode her before I went away. I left her in old Sammy's charge, and he has been riding her every day."

"And glad enough to do it, I am sure," said she, "for I have heard him say that the things he hates most in this world are dead legs. 'When I can't use mine,' he said, 'let me have some others that are alive.' This is such a pretty creature," she added, as Clewe was looking about for some place to which he might tie his animal, "that I have a great mind to learn to ride myself!"

"A woman on a horse would be a queer sight," said he; and

with this they went into the house.

The conference that morning in Mrs. Raleigh's library was a long and somewhat anxious one. For several years the money of the Raleigh estate had been freely and generously expended upon the enterprises in hand at the Sardis Works, but so far nothing of important profit had resulted from the operations. Many things had been carried on satisfactorily and successfully to various stages, but nothing had been finished; and now the two partners had to admit that the work which Clewe had expected to begin immediately upon his return from Europe must be postponed.

Still, there was no sign of discouragement in the voices or the faces—it may be said, in the souls—of the man and woman who sat there talking across a table. He was as full of hope as ever he was, and she as full of faith.

They were an interesting couple to look upon. He, dark, a little hollow in the cheeks, a slight line or two of anxiety in the forehead, a handsome, well-cut mouth, without beard, and a frame somewhat spare but strong; a man of graceful but unaffected action, dressed in a riding-coat, breeches, and leather leggings. She, her cheeks colored with earnest purpose, her gray eyes rather larger than usual as she looked up from the paper where she had been calculating, was dressed in the simple artistic fashion of the day. The falling folds of the semi-clinging fabrics accommodated themselves well to a figure which even at that moment of rest suggested latent energy and activity.

"If we have to wait for the Artesian ray," she said, "we must try to carry out something else. People are watching us, talking of us, expecting something of us; we must give them something. Now the question is, what shall that be?"

"The way I look at it is this," said her companion. "For a

　　　　　Frank R. Stockton

long time you have been watching and waiting and expecting something, and it is time that I should give you something; now the question is—"

"Not at all," said she, interrupting. "You arrogate too much to yourself. I don't expect you to give anything to me. We are working together, and it is both of us who must give this poor old world something to satisfy it for a while, until we can disclose to it that grand discovery, grander than anything that it has ever even imagined. I want to go on talking about it, but I shall not do it; we must keep our minds tied down to some present purpose. Now, Mr. Clewe, what is there that we can take up and carry on immediately? Can it be the great shell?"

Clewe shook his head.

"No," said he; "that is progressing admirably, but many things are necessary before we can experiment with it."

"Since you were away," said she, "I have often been down to the works to look at it, but everything about it seems to go so slowly. However, I suppose it will go fast enough when it is finished."

"Yes," said he. "I hope it will go fast enough to overturn the artillery of the world; but, as you say, don't let us talk about the things for which we must wait. I will carefully consider everything that is in operation, and to-morrow I will suggest something with which we can go on."

"After all," said she, as they stood together before parting, "I cannot take my mind from the Artesian ray."

"Nor can I," he answered; "but for the present we must put our hands to work at something else."

The Artesian ray, of which these two spoke, was an invention upon which Roland Clewe had been experimenting for a long time, and which was and had been the object of his labors and studies while in Europe. In the first decade of the century it had been generally supposed that the X ray, or cathode ray, had been developed and applied to the utmost extent of its capability. It was used in surgery and in mechanical arts, and in many varieties of scientific operations, but no considerable advance in its line of application had been recognized for a quarter of a century. But Roland Clewe had come to believe in the existence of a photic force, somewhat similar to the cathode ray, but of infinitely greater significance and importance to the searcher after physical truth. Simply described, his discovery was a powerful ray produced by a new combination of electric lights, which would penetrate down into the earth, passing through all substances which it met in its way, and illuminating and disclosing everything through which it passed.

All matter likely to be found beneath the surface of the earth in that part of the country had been experimented upon by Clewe, and nothing had resisted the penetrating and illuminating influence of his ray—well called Artesian ray, for it was intended to bore into the bowels of the earth. After making many minor trials of the force and powers of his light, Roland Clewe had undertaken the construction of a massive apparatus, by which he believed a ray could be generated which, little by little, perhaps foot by foot, would penetrate into the earth and light up everything between the farthest point it had attained and the lenses of his machine. That is to say, he hoped to produce a long hole of light about three feet in diameter and as deep as it was possible to make it descend, in which he could see all the various strata and deposits of which the earth is composed. How far he could send down this piercing cylinder of light he did not allow himself to consider. With a small and imperfect machine he

Frank R. Stockton

had seen several feet into the ground; with a great and powerful apparatus, such as he was now constructing, why should he not look down below the deepest point to which man's knowledge had ever reached? Down so far that he must follow his descending light with a telescope; down, down until he had discovered the hidden secrets of the earth!

The peculiar quality of this light, which gave it its great preeminence over all other penetrating rays, was the power it possessed of illuminating an object; passing through it; rendering it transparent and invisible; illuminating the opaque substance it next met in its path, and afterwards rendering that transparent. If the rocks and earth in the cylindrical cavities of light which Clewe had already produced in his experiments had actually been removed with pickaxes and shovels, the lighted hole a few feet in depth could not have appeared more real, the bottom and sides of the little well could not have been revealed more sharply and distinctly; and yet there was no hole in the ground, and if one should try to put his foot into the lighted perforation he would find it as solid as any other part of the earth.

CHAPTER IV

THE MISSION OF SAMUEL BLOCK

Not far from the works at Sardis there was a large pond, which was formed by the damming of a stream which at this point ran between high hills. In order to obtain a sufficient depth of water for his marine experiments, Roland Clewe had built an unusually high and strong dam, and this body of water, which was called the lake, widened out considerably behind the dam and stretched back for more than half a mile.

He was standing on the shore of this lake, early the next morning, in company with several workmen, examining a curious-looking vessel which was moored near by, when Margaret Raleigh came walking towards him. When he saw her he left the men and went to meet her.

"You could not wait until I came to your house to tell you what I was going to do?" he said, smiling.

"No," she answered, "I could not. The Artesian ray kept me awake nearly all night, and I felt that I must quiet my mind as soon as I could by giving it something real and tangible to take hold of. Now what is it that you are going to do? Anything in the ship line?"

"Yes," said he, "it is something in that line. But let us walk

Frank R. Stockton

back a little; I am not quite ready to tell the men everything. I have been thinking," he said, as they moved together from the lake, "of that practical enterprise which we must take up and finish, in order to justify ourselves to the public and those who have in various ways backed up our enterprises, and I have concluded that the best thing I can do is to carry out my plan of going to the north pole."

"What!" she exclaimed. "You are not going to try to do that —you, yourself?" And as she spoke, her voice trembled a little.

"Yes," said he, "I thought I would go myself, or else send Sammy."

She laughed.

"Ridiculous!" said she. "Send Sammy Block! You are joking?"

"No," said he, "I am not. I have been planning the expedition, and I think Sammy would be an excellent man to take charge of it. I might go part of the way—at least, far enough to start him—and I could so arrange matters that Sammy would have no difficulty in finishing the expedition, but I do not think that I could give up all the time that such an enterprise deserves. It is not enough to merely find the pole; one should stay there and make observations which would be of service."

"But if Sammy finishes the journey himself," she said, "his will be the glory."

"Let him have it," replied Clewe. "If my method of arctic exploration solves the great problem of the pole, I shall be satisfied with the glory I get from the conception. The mere journey to the northern end of the earth's axis is of slight importance. I shall be glad to have Sammy go first, and have as many follow him as may choose to travel in that direction."

"Yet it is a great achievement," said she. "I would give much to be the first human being who has placed his foot upon the north pole."

"You would get it wet, I am afraid," said Clewe, smiling; "but that is not the kind of glory I crave. If I can help a man to go there, I shall be very willing to do so, provided he will make me a favorable report of his discoveries."

"Tell me all about it," she said—"when will you start? How many will go?"

"There is some work to be done on that boat," said he. "Let me set the men at it, and then we will go into the office, and I will lay everything before you."

When they were seated in a quiet little room attached to one of the large buildings, Roland Clewe made ready to describe his proposed arctic expedition to his partner, in whose mind the wonderful enterprise had entered, driving out the disturbing thoughts of the Artesian ray.

"You have told me about it before," said she, "but I am not quite sure that I have it all straight in my mind. You will go, I suppose, in a submarine boat—that is, whoever goes will go in it?"

"Yes," said he, "for part of the way. My plan is to proceed in an ordinary vessel as far north as Cape Tariff, taking the Dipsey, my submarine boat, in tow. The exploring party, with the necessary stores and instruments, will embark on the Dipsey, but before they start they will make a telegraphic connection with the station at Cape Tariff. The Dipsey will

Frank R. Stockton

carry one of those light, portable cables, which will be wound on a drum in her hold, and this will be paid out as she proceeds on her way. Thus, you see, by means of the cable from Cape Tariff to St. Johns, we can be in continual communication with Sammy, no matter where he may go; for there is no reason to suppose that the ocean in those northern regions is too deep to allow the successful placing of a telegraphic cable.

"My plan is a very simple one, but as we have not talked it over for some time, I will describe it in full. All explorers who have tried to get to the north pole have met with the same bad fortune. They could not pass over the vast and awful regions of ice which lay between them and the distant point at which they aimed; the deadly ice-land was always too much for them; they died or they turned back.

"When flying-machines were brought to supposed perfection, some twenty years ago, it was believed that the pole would easily be reached, but there were always the wild and wicked winds, in which no steering apparatus could be relied upon. We may steer and manage our vessels in the fiercest storms at sea, but when the ocean moves in one great tidal wave our rudders are of no avail. Everything rushes on together, and our strongest ships are cast high upon the land.

"So it happened to the Canadian Bagne, who went in 1927 in the best flying-ship ever made, and which it was supposed could be steadily kept upon its way without regard to the influence of the strongest winds; but a great hurricane came down from the north, as if square miles of atmosphere were driving onward in a steady mass, and hurled him and his ship against an iceberg, and nothing of his vessel but pieces of wood and iron, which the bears could not eat, was ever seen again. This was the last polar expedition of that sort, or any sort; but my plan is so easy of accomplishment—at least, so it seems to me—and so devoid of risk and danger, that it amazes me that it has never been tried before. In fact, if I had not thought that it would be such a comparatively easy thing to go to the pole, I believe I should have been there long ago; but I have always considered that it could be done at some season when more difficult and engrossing projects were not pressing upon me.

"What I propose to do is to sink down below the bottom of the ice in the arctic regions, and then to proceed in a direct line northward to the pole. The distance between the lower portions of the ice and the bottom of the Arctic Ocean I believe to be quite sufficient to allow me all the room needed for navigation. I do not think it necessary to even consider the contingency of the greatest iceberg or floe reaching the bottom of the arctic waters; consequently, without trouble or danger, the Dipsey can make a straight course for the extreme north.

"By means of the instruments the Dipsey will carry it will be comparatively easy to determine the position of the pole, and before this point is reached I believe she will find herself in an open sea, where she may rise to the surface. But if this should not be the case, a comparatively thin place in the ice will be chosen, and a great opening blown through it by means of an ascensional shell, several of which she will carry. She will then rise to the surface of the water in this opening, and the necessary operations will be carried on."

"Mr. Clewe," said Margaret Raleigh, "the thing is so terrible I cannot bear to think of it. The Dipsey may have to sail hundreds and hundreds of miles under the ice, shut in as if an awful lid were put over her. No matter what happened down there, she could not come up and get out; it would be the same thing as having a vast sky of ice stretched out above one. I should think the very idea of it would make people shudder and die."

"Oh, it is not so bad as all that," answered Clewe. "There is nothing so dear to the marine explorer as plenty of water, and plenty of room to sail in, and under the ice the Dipsey will find all that."

"But there are so many dangers," said she, "that you cannot provide against in advance."

"That is very true," said he, "but I have thought so much about them, and I have studied and consulted so much about them, that I think I have provided against all the dangers we have reason to expect. To me the whole business seems like very plain, straightforward sailing."

"It may seem so here," said Margaret Raleigh, "but it will be quite another thing out under the arctic ice."

Preparations for the expedition were pushed forward as rapidly as possible, and Clewe would have been delighted to make this voyage into the unseen regions of the nether ice, but he knew that it was his duty not to lose time or to risk his life when he was on the brink of a discovery far more wonderful, far more important to the world, than the finding of the pole. Therefore he determined that he would go with the expedition no farther than the point where the ice would prevent the farther progress of the vessel in which they would sail from New York.

It was not to be supposed that Roland Clewe intended to intrust such an expedition to the absolute command of such a man as old Samuel Block. There would be on board the Dipsey an electrician who had long been preparing himself for this expedition; there were to be other scientific men; there would be a submarine engineer, and such minor officers and assistants as would be necessary; but Clewe wanted some one who would represent him, who could be trusted to act in his place in case of success or of failure, who could be thoroughly depended upon should a serious emergency arise. Such a man was Samuel Block, and, somewhat strange to say, old Sammy was perfectly willing to go to the pole. He was always ready for anything within bounds of his duty, and those bounds included everything which Mr. Clewe wished done.

Sammy was an old-fashioned man, and therefore, in talking over arrangements with Roland Clewe, he insisted upon having a sailor in the party.

"In old times," said he, "when I was a young man, nobody ever thought of settin' out on any kind of sea-voyagin' without havin' a sailor along. The fact is, they used to be pretty much all sailors."

"But in this expedition," said Clewe, "a sailor would be out of place. One of your old-fashioned mariners would not know what to do under the water. Submarine voyaging is an entirely different profession from that of the old-time navigator."

"I know all that," said Sammy. "I know how everything is a machine nowadays; but I shall never forget what a glorious thing it was to sail on the sea with the wind blowin' and the water curlin' beneath your keel. I lived on the coast, and used to go out whenever I had a chance, but things is mightily changed nowadays. Just think of that yacht-race in England the other day—a race between two electric yachts, with a couple of vessels ploughin' along to windward carryin' between 'em a board fence thirty feet high to keep the wind off the yachts and give 'em both smooth water and equal chance. I can't get used to that sort of thing, and I tell you, sir, that if I am goin' on a voyage to the pole, I want to have a sailor along. If everything goes all right, we must come to the top of the water some time, and then we ought to have at least one man who understands surface navigation."

"All right," said Clewe; "get your sailor."

"I've got my eye on him; he's a Cape Cod man, and he's not so very old either. When he was a boy people went about in ships with sails, and even after he grew up Cap'n Jim was a great feller to manage a catboat; for things has moved slower on the Cape than in many parts of the country."

So Captain Jim Hubbell was engaged as sailor to the expedition; and when he came on to Sardis and looked over the Dipsey he expressed a general opinion of her construction and capabilities which indicated a disposition on his part to send her, and all others fashioned after her plan, to depths a great deal lower than ever had been contemplated by their inventors. Still, as he wanted very much to go to the pole if it was possible that he could get there, and as the wages offered him were exceedingly liberal, Captain Jim enlisted, in the party. His duties were to begin when the Dipsey floated on the surface of the sea like a commonsense craft.

A day or two before the expedition was ready to start, Roland Clewe was very much surprised one morning by a visit from Sammy's wife, Mrs. Sarah Block, who lost no time in informing him that she had made up her mind to accompany her husband on the perilous voyage he was about to make.

"You!" said Clewe. "You could not go on such an expedition as that!"

"If Sammy goes, I go," said Mrs. Block. "If it is dangerous for me, it is dangerous for him. I have been tryin' to get sense enough in his head to make him stay at home, but I can't do it; so I have made up my mind that I go with him or he don't go. We have travelled together on top of the land, and we have travelled together on top of the water, and if there's to be travellin' under the water, why then we travel together all the same. If Sammy goes polin', I go polin'. I think he's a fool to do it; but if he's goin' to be a fool, I am goin' to be a fool. And as for my bein' in the way, you needn't think of that, Mr. Clewe. I can cook for the livin', I can take care of the sick, and I can sew up the dead in shrouds."

"All right, Mrs. Block," said Clewe. "If you insist on it, and Sammy is willing, you may go; but I will beg of you not to say anything about the third class of good offices which you propose to perform for the party, for it might cast a gloom over some of the weaker-minded."

"Cast a gloom!" said Mrs. Block. "If all I hear is true, there will be a general gloom over everything that will be like havin' a black pocket-handkercher tied over your head, and I don't know that anything I could say would make that gloom more gloomier."

When Margaret Raleigh parted with Clewe on the deck of the Go Lightly, the large electric vessel which was to tow the Dipsey up to the limits of navigable Northern waters, she knew he must make a long journey, nearly twice as far as the voyage to England, before she could hear from him; but when he arrived at Cape Tariff, a point far up on the northwestern coast of Greenland, she would hear from him; for from this point there was telegraphic communication with the rest of the world. There was a little station there, established by some commercial companies, and their agent was a telegraph-operator.

The passage from New York to Cape Tariff was an uneventful one, and when Clewe disembarked at the lonely Greenland station he was greeted by a long message from Mrs. Raleigh, the principal import of which was that on no account must he allow himself to be persuaded to go on the submarine voyage of the Dipsey. On his part, Clewe had no desire to make any change in his plans. During all the long voyage northward his heart had been at Sardis.

The Dipsey was a comparatively small vessel, but it afforded comfortable accommodations for a dozen or more people, and there was room for all the stores which would be needed for a year. She was furnished, besides, with books and every useful and convenient contrivance which had been thought desirable for her peculiar expedition.

When everything was ready, Roland Clewe took leave of the officers, the crew, and the passenger on board the Dipsey, and the last-mentioned, as she shook hands with him, shed tears.

"It seems to me like a sort of a congregational suicide, Mr. Clewe," said she. "And it can't even be said that all the members are doin' it of their own accord, for I am not. If Sammy did not go, I would not, but if he does, I do, and there's the end of that; and I suppose it won't be very much longer before there's the end of all of us. I hope you will tell Mrs. Raleigh that I sent my best love to her with my last words; for even if I was to see her again, it would seem to me like beginning all over again, and this would be the end of this part of my life all the same. What I hope and pray for is that none of the party may die of any kind of a disease before the rest all go to their end together; for remains on board an under-water vessel is somethin' which mighty few nerves would be able to stand."

When all farewells had been said, Mr. Clewe went on board the Go Lightly, on the deck of which were her officers and men and the few inhabitants of the station, and then the plate-glass hatchways of the Dipsey were tightly closed, and she began to sink, until she entirely disappeared below the surface of the water, leaving above her a little floating glass globe, connected with her by an electric wire.

As the Dipsey went under the sea, this little globe followed her on the surface, and the Go Lightly immediately began to move after her. This arrangement had been made, as Clewe wished to follow the Dipsey for a time, in order to see if everything was working properly with her. She kept on a straight course, flashing a light into the little globe every now and then; and finally, after meeting some floating ice, she shattered the globe with an explosion, which was the signal agreed upon to show that all was well, and that the Dipsey had started off alone on the submarine voyage to the pole.

Roland Clewe gazed out over the wide stretch of dark-green waves and glistening crests, where nothing could be seen which indicated life except a distant, wearily-flapping sea bird, and then, turning his back upon the pole, he made preparations for his return voyage to New York, at which port he might expect to receive direct news from Sammy Block and his companions.

Frank R. Stockton

CHAPTER V

UNDER WATER

When the Dipsey, the little submarine vessel which had started to make its way to the north pole under the ice of the arctic regions, had sunk out of sight under the waters, it carried a very quiet and earnestly observant party. Every one seemed anxious to know what would happen next, and all those whose duties would allow them to do so gathered under the great skylight in the upper deck, and gazed upward at the little glass bulb on the surface of the water, which they were towing by means of an electric wire; and every time a light was flashed into this bulb it seemed to them as if they were for an instant reunited to that vast open world outside of the ocean. When at last the glass globe was exploded, as a signal that the Dipsey had cut loose from all ties which connected her with the outer world, they saw through the water above them the flash and the sparks, and then all was darkness.

The interior of the submarine vessel was brightly lighted by electric lamps, and the souls of the people inside of her soon began to brighten under the influence of their work and the interest they took in their novel undertaking; there was, however, one exception—the soul of Mrs. Block did not brighten.

Mrs. Sarah Block was a peculiar person; she was her husband's second wife, and was about forty years of age. Her family were country people, farmers, and her life as a child was passed among folk as old-fashioned as if they had lived in the past century, and had brought their old-fashioned ideas with them into this. But Sarah did not wish to be old-fashioned. She sympathized with the social movements of the day; she believed in inventions and progress; she went to school and studied a great deal which her parents never heard of, and which she very promptly forgot. When she grew up she wore the widest hoop-skirts; she was one of the first to use an electric spinning-wheel; and when she took charge of her father's house, she it was who banished to the garret the old-fashioned sewing-machine, and the bicycles on which some of the older members of the family once used to ride. She tried to persuade her father to use a hot-air plough, and to give up the practice of keeping cows in an age when milk and butter were considered not only unnecessary, but injurious to human health. When she married Samuel Block, then a man of forty-five, she really thought she did so because he was a person of progressive ideas, but the truth was she married him because he loved her, and because he did it in an honest, old-fashioned way.

In her inner soul Sarah was just as old-fashioned as anybody—she had been born so, and she had never changed. Endeavor as she might to make herself believe that she was a woman of modern thought and feeling, her soul was truly in sympathy with the social fashions and customs in which she had been brought up; and those to which she was trying to educate herself were on the outside of her, never a part of her, but always the objects of her aspirations. These aspirations she believed to be principles. She tried to set her mind upon the unfolding revelations of the era, as young women in her grandfather's day used to try to set their minds upon Browning. When Sarah told Mr. Clewe that she was going on the Dipsey because she would not let her husband go by himself, she did so because she was ashamed to say that she was in such sympathy with the great scientific movements of the day that she thought it was her duty to associate herself with one of them; but while she thought she was lying in the line of high principle, she was in fact expressing the truthful affection of her old-fashioned nature —a nature she was always endeavoring to keep out of sight, but which from its dark corner ruled her life.

She had an old-fashioned temper, which delighted in censoriousness. The more interest she took in anything, the more alive was she to its defects. She tried to be a good member of her church, but she said sharp things of the congregation.

No electrical illumination could brighten the soul of Mrs. Block. She moved about the little vessel with a clouded countenance. She was impressed with the feeling that something was wrong, even now at the beginning, although of course she could not be expected to know what it was.

At the bows, and in various places at the sides of the vessel, and even in the bottom, were large plates of heavy glass, through which the inmates could look out into the water, and there streamed forward into the quiet depths of the ocean a great path of light, proceeding from a powerful searchlight in the bow. By this light any object in the water could be seen some time before reaching it; but to guard more thoroughly against the most dreaded obstacle they feared to meet— down-reaching masses of ice—a hydraulic thermometer, mounted on a little submarine vessel connected with the Dipsey by wires, preceded her a long distance ahead. Impelled and guided by the batteries of the larger vessel, this little thermometer-boat would send back instant tidings of any changes in temperature in the water occasioned by the proximity of ice. To prevent sinking too deep, a heavy lead, on which were several electric buttons, hung far below the Dipsey, ready at all times, day or night, to give notice if she came too near the reefs and sands of the bottom of the Arctic Ocean.

The steward had just announced that the first meal on board the Dipsey was ready for the officers' mess, when Mrs. Block suddenly rushed into the cabin.

"Look here, Sammy," she exclaimed; "I want you, or somebody who knows more than you do, to tell me how the people on this vessel are goin' to get air to breathe with. It has just struck me that when we have breathed up all the air that's inside, we will simply suffocate, just as if we were drowned outside a boat instead of inside; and for my part I can't see any difference, except in one case we keep dry and in the other we are wet."

"More than that, madam," said Mr. Gibbs, the Master Electrician, who, in fact, occupied the rank of first officer of the vessel; "if we are drowned outside in the open water we shall be food for fishes, whereas if we suffocate inside the vessel we shall only be food for reflection, if anybody ever finds us."

"You did not come out expectin' that, I hope?" said Mrs. Block. "I thought something would happen when we started, but I never supposed we would run short of air."

"Don't bother yourself about that, Sarah," said Sammy. "We'll have all the air we want; of course we would not start without thinkin' of that."

"I don't know," said Sarah. "It's very seldom that men start off anywhere without forgettin' somethin'."

"Let us take our seats, Mrs. Block," said Mr. Gibbs, "and I will set your mind at rest on the air point. There are a great many machines and mechanical arrangements on board here which of course you don't understand, but which I shall take great pleasure in explaining to you whenever you want to learn something about them. Among them are two great metal contrivances, outside the Dipsey and near her bows, which open into the water, and also communicate with the inside of her hull. These are called electric gills, and they separate air from the water around us in a manner somewhat resembling the way in which a fish's gills act. They continually send in air enough to supply us not only with all we need for breathing, but with enough to raise us to the surface of the water whenever we choose to produce it in sufficient quantities."

"I am glad to hear it," said Mrs. Block, "and I hope the machines will never get out of order. But I should think that sort of air, made fresh from the water, would be very damp. It's very different from the air we are used to, which is warmed by the sun and properly aired."

"Aired air seems funny to me," remarked Sammy.

There was fascination, not at all surprising, about the great glass lights in the Dipsey, and whenever a man was off duty he was pretty sure to be at one of these windows if he could get there. At first Mrs. Block was afraid to look out of any of them. It made her blood creep, she said, to stare out into all that solemn water. For the first two days, when she could get no one to talk to her, she passed most of her time sitting in the cabin, holding in one of her hands a dustbrush, and in the other a farmer's almanac. She did not use the brush, nor did she read the almanac, but they reminded her of home and the world which was real.

But when she did make up her mind to look out of the windows, she became greatly interested, especially at the bow, where she could gaze out into the water illuminated by the long lane of light thrown out by the search-light. Here she continually imagined she saw things, and sometimes greatly startled the men on lookout by her exclamations. Once she thought she saw a floating corpse, but fortunately it was Sammy who was by her when she proclaimed her discovery, and he did not believe in any such nonsense, suggesting that it might have been some sort of a fish. After that the idea of fish filled the mind of Mrs. Block, and she set herself to work to search in an encyclopaedia which was on board for descriptions of fishes which inhabited the depths of the arctic seas. To meet a whale, she thought, would be very bad, but then a whale is clumsy and soft; a sword-fish was what she most dreaded. A sword-fish running his sword through one of the glass windows, and perhaps coming in himself along with the water, sent a chill down her back every time she thought about it and talked about it.

"You needn't be afraid of sword-fishes," said Captain Jim Hubbell. "They don't fancy the cold water we are sailin' in; and as to whales, don't you know, madam, there ain't no more of 'em?"

"No more whales!" exclaimed Sarah. "I have heard about 'em all my life!"

"Oh, you can read and hear about 'em easy enough," replied Captain Jim, "but you nor nobody else will ever see none of 'em ag'in—at least, in this part of the world. Sperm-whales began gittin' scarce when I was a boy, and pretty soon there was nothin' left but bow-head or right whales, that tried to keep out of the way of human bein's by livin' far up North; but when they came to shootin' 'em with cannons which would carry three or four miles, the whale's day was up, and he got scarcer and scarcer, until he faded out altogether. There was a British vessel, the Barkright, that killed two bow-head whales in 1935, north of Melville Island, but since that time there hasn't been a whale seen in all the arctic waters. I have heard that said by sailors, and I have read

Frank R. Stockton

about it. They have all been killed, and nothin' left of 'em but the skeletons that's in the museums."

Mrs. Block shuddered. "It would be terrible to meet a livin' one, and yet it is an awful thought to think that they are all dead and gone," said she.

CHAPTER VI

VOICES FROM THE POLAR SEAS

Although Sammy Block and his companions were not only far up among the mysteries of the region of everlasting ice, and were sunk out of sight, so that their vessel had become one of these mysteries, it was still perfectly possible for them to communicate, by means of the telegraphic wire which was continually unrolling astern, with people all over the world. But this communication was a matter which required great judgment and caution, and it had been a subject of very careful consideration by Roland Clewe.

When he had returned to Cape Tariff, after parting with the Dipsey, he had received several messages from Sammy, which assured him that the submarine voyage was proceeding satisfactorily. But when he went on board the Go Lightly and started homeward, he would be able to hear nothing more from the submarine voyagers until he reached St. John's, Newfoundland—the first place at which his vessel would touch. Of course constant communication with Sardis would be kept up, but this communication might be the source of great danger to the plans of Roland Clewe. Whatever messages of importance came from the depths of the arctic regions he wished to come only to him or to Mrs. Raleigh. He had contrived a telegraphic cipher, known only to Mrs. Raleigh, Sammy, and two officers of the Dipsey, and, to insure secrecy, Sammy had been strictly enjoined to send no information in any other way than in this cipher.

For years there had been men, both in America and in Europe, who had been watching with jealous scrutiny the inventions and researches of Roland Clewe, and he well understood that if they should discover his processes and plans before they were brought to successful completion he must expect to be robbed of many of the results of his labors. The first news that came to him on his recent return to America had been the tale told by Sammy Block, of the man in the air who had been endeavoring to peer down into his lens-house, and he had heard of other attempts of this kind. Therefore it was that the telegraphic instrument on the Dipsey had been given into the sole charge of Samuel Block, who had become a very capable operator, and who could be relied upon to send no news over his wire which could give serviceable information to the operators along the line from Cape Tariff to Sardis, New Jersey.

But Clewe did not in the least desire that Margaret Raleigh should be kept waiting until he came back from the arctic regions for news from the expedition, which she as well as himself had sent out into the unknown North. Consequently Samuel Block had been told that he might communicate with Mrs. Raleigh as soon and as often as he pleased, remembering always to be careful never to send any word which might reveal anything to the detriment of his employers. When a message should be received on board the Dipsey that Mr. Clewe was ready to communicate with her, frequent reports were expected from the Master Electrician, but it would be Sammy who would unlock the cover which had been placed over the instrument.

Before he retired to his bunk on the first night on board the Dipsey, Sammy thought it proper to send a message to Mrs. Raleigh. He had not telegraphed before because he knew that

Mr. Clewe would communicate fully before he left Cape Tariff.

Margaret Raleigh had gone to bed late, and had been lying for an hour or two unable to sleep, so busy was her mind with the wonderful things which were happening in the far-away polar regions—strange and awful things—in which she had such a direct and lively interest. She had heard, from Roland Clewe, of the successful beginning of the Dipsey's voyage, and before she had gone to her chamber she had received a last message from him on leaving Cape Tariff; and now, as she lay there in her bed, her whole soul was occupied with thoughts of that little party of people—some of them so well known to her—all of them sent out upon this perilous and frightful expedition by her consent and assistance, and now left alone to work their way through the dread and silent waters that underlie the awful ice regions of the pole. She felt that so long as she had a mind she could not help thinking of them, and so long as she thought of them she could not sleep.

Suddenly there was a ring at the door, which made her start and spring from her bed, and shortly a telegraphic message was brought to her by a maid. It was from the depths of the Arctic Ocean, and read as follows:

"Getting on very well. No motion. Not cold. Slight rheumatism in Sarah's shoulder. Wants to know which side of plasters you gave her goes next skin,

"SAMUEL BLOCK."

An hour afterwards there flashed farther northward than ever current from a battery had gone before an earnest, cordial, almost affectionate message from Margaret Raleigh to Sarah Block, and it concluded with the information that it was the rough side of the plasters which should go next to the skin.

After that Mrs. Raleigh went to bed with a peaceful mind and slept soundly.

Frequent communications, always of a friendly or domestic nature, passed between the polar sea and Sardis during the next few days. Mrs. Raleigh would have telegraphed a good deal more than she did had it not been for the great expense from Sardis to Cape Tariff, and Sarah Block was held in restraint, not by pecuniary considerations, but by Sammy's sense of the fitness of things. He nearly always edited her messages, even when he consented to send them. One communication he positively refused to transmit. She came to him in a great flurry.

"Sammy," said she, "I have just found out something, and I can't rest until I have told Mrs. Raleigh. I won't mention it here, because it might frighten some people into fits and spasms. Sammy, do you know there are thirteen people on board this boat?"

"Sarah Block!" ejaculated her husband, "what in the name of common-sense are you talkin' about? What earthly difference can it make whether there are thirteen people on this vessel or twelve? And if it did make any difference, what are you goin' to do about it? Do you expect anybody to get out?"

"Of course I don't," replied Sarah; "although there are some of them that would not have come in if I had had my say about it; but as Mrs. Raleigh is one of the owners, and such a good friend to you and me, Sammy, it is our duty to let her know what dreadful bad luck we are carryin' with us."

"Don't you suppose she knows how many people are aboard?" said Sammy.

"Of course she knows; but she don't consider what it means, or we wouldn't all have been here. It is her right to know,

Sammy. Perhaps she might order us to go back to Cape Tariff and put somebody ashore."

In his heart Samuel Block believed that if this course were adopted he was pretty sure who would be put on shore, if a vote were taken by officers and crew; but he was too wise to say anything upon this point, and contented himself with positively refusing to send southward any news of the evil omen.

The next day Mrs. Block felt that she must speak upon the subject or perish, and she asked Mr. Gibbs what he thought of there being thirteen people on board.

"Madam," said he, "these signs lose all their powers above the seventieth parallel of latitude. In fact, none of them have ever been known to come true above sixty-eight degrees and forty minutes, and we are a good deal higher than that, you know."

Sarah made no answer, but she told her husband afterwards that she thought that Mr. Gibbs had his mind so full of electricity that it had no room for old-fashioned common-sense. It did not do to sneer at signs and portents. Among the earliest things she remembered was a story which had been told her of her grandmother's brother, who was the thirteenth passenger in an omnibus when he was a young man, and who died that very night, having slipped off the back step, where he was obliged to stand, and fractured his skull.

At last there came a day when a message in cipher from Roland Clewe delivered itself on board the Dipsey, and from that moment a hitherto unknown sense of security seemed to pervade the minds of officers and crew. To be sure, there was no good reason for this, for if disaster should overtake them, or even threaten them, there was no submarine boat ready to send to their rescue; and if there had been, it would be long, long before such aid could reach them; but still, they were comforted, encouraged, and cheered. Now, if anything happened, they could send news of it to the man in whom they all trusted, and through him to their homes, and whatever their far-away friends had to say to them could be said without reserve.

There was nothing yet of definite scientific importance to report, but the messages of the Master Electrician were frequent and long, regardless of expense, and, so far as her husband would permit her, Sarah Block informed Mrs. Raleigh of the discouragements and dangers which awaited this expedition. It must be said, however, that Mrs. Block never proposed to send back one word which should indicate that she was in favor of the abandonment of the expedition, or of her retirement from it should opportunity allow. She had set out for the north pole because Sammy was going there, and the longer she went "polin'" with him, the stronger became her curiosity to see the pole and to know what it looked like.

The Dipsey was not expected to be, under any circum- stances, a swift vessel, and now, retarded by her outside attachments, she moved but slowly under the waters. The telegraphic wire which she laid as she proceeded was the thinnest and lightest submarine cable ever manufactured, but the mass of it was of great weight, and as it found its way to the bottom it much retarded the progress of the vessel, which moved more slowly than was absolutely necessary, for fear of breaking this connection with the living world.

Onward, but a few knots an hour, the Dipsey moved like a fish in the midst of the sea. The projectors of the enterprise had a firm belief that there was a channel from Baffin's Bay into an open polar sea, which would be navigable if its entrance were not blocked up by ice, and on this belief were based all their hopes of success. So the explorers pressed steadily onward, always with an anxious lookout above them for fear of striking the overhanging ice, always with an anxious lookout below for fear of dangers which might loom up from the bottom, always with an anxious lookout starboard for fear of running against the foundations of Greenland, always with an anxious lookout to port for fear of striking the groundwork of the unknown land to the west, and always keeping a lookout in every direction for whatever revelation these unknown waters might choose to make to them.

Captain Jim Hubbell had no sympathy with the methods of navigation practised on board the Dipsey. So long as he could not go out on deck and take his noon observations, he did not believe it would be possible for him to know exactly where his vessel was; but he accepted the situation, and objected to none of the methods of the scientific navigators.

"It's a mighty simple way of sailin'," he said to Sammy. "As long as there's water to sail in, you have just got to git on a line of longitude—it doesn't matter what line, so long as there's water ahead of you—and keep there; and so long as you steer due north, always takin' care not to switch off to the magnetic pole, of course you will keep there; and as all lines of longitude come to the same point at last, and as that's the point you are sailin' for, of course, if you can keep on that line of longitude as long as it lasts, it follows that you are bound to git there. If you come to any place on this line of longitude where there's not enough water to sail her, you have got to stop her; and then, if you can't see any way of goin' ahead on another line of longitude, you can put her about and go out of this on the same line of longitude that you came up into it on, and so you may expect to find a way clear. It's mighty simple sailin'—regular spellin' book navigation—but it isn't the right thing."

"It seems that way, Cap'n Jim," said Sammy, "and I expect

there's a long stretch of underwater business ahead of us yet, but still we can't tell. How do we know that we will not get up some mornin' soon and look out of the upper skylight and see nothin' but water over us and daylight beyond that?"

"When we do that, Sammy," said Captain Jim, "then I'll truly believe I'm on a v'yage!"

CHAPTER VII

GOOD NEWS GOES FROM SARDIS

When Roland Clewe, after a voyage from Cape Tariff which would have been tedious to him no matter how short it had been, arrived at Sardis, his mind was mainly occupied with the people he had left behind him engulfed in the arctic seas, but this important subject did not prevent him from also giving attention to the other great object upon which his soul was bent. At St. John's, and at various points on his journey from there, he had received messages from the Dipsey, so that he knew that so far all was well, and when he met Mrs. Raleigh she had much to tell him of what might have been called the domestic affairs of the little vessel.

But while keeping himself in touch, as it were, with the polar regions, Roland Clewe longed to use the means he believed he possessed of peering into the subterranean mysteries of the earth beneath him. Work on the great machine by which he would generate his Artesian ray had been going on very satisfactorily, and there was every reason to believe that he would soon be able to put it into operation.

He had found Margaret Raleigh a different woman from what she had been when he left her.

The absence had been short, but the change in her was very

Frank R. Stockton

perceptible. She was quieter; she was more intent. She had always taken a great interest in his undertakings, but now that interest not only seemed to be deepened, but it was clouded by a certain anxiety. She had been an ardent, cheerful, and hopeful co-worker with him, so far as she was able to do so; but now, although she was quite as ardent, the cheerfulness had disappeared, and she did not allude to the hopefulness.

But this did not surprise Clewe; he thought it the most natural thing in the world; for that polar expedition was enough to cloud the spirits of any woman who had an active part and share in it, and who was bound to feel that much of the responsibility of it rested upon her. At times this responsibility rested very heavily upon himself. But if thoughts of that little submerged party at the desolate end of the world came to him as he sat in his comfortable chair, and a cold dread shot through him, as it was apt to do at such times, he would hurriedly step to his telegraphic instrument, and when he had heard from Sammy Block that all was well with them, his spirits would rise again, and he would go on with his work with a soul cheered and encouraged.

But good news from the North did not appear to cheer and encourage the soul of Mrs. Raleigh. She seemed anxious and troubled even after she had heard it.

"Mr. Clewe," said she, when he had called upon her the next morning after his return, "suppose you were to hear bad news from the Dipsey, or were to hear nothing at all—were to get no answer to your messages—what would you do?"

His face grew troubled.

"That is a terrible question," he said. "It is one I have often asked myself; but there is no satisfactory answer to it. Of course, as I have told myself and have told you, there seems no reason to expect a disaster. There are no storms in the quiet depths in which the Dipsey is sailing. Ice does not sink down from the surface, and even if a floating iceberg should turn over, as they sometimes do in the more open sea, the Dipsey will keep low enough to avoid such danger. In fact, I feel almost sure that if she should meet with any obstacle which would prevent her from keeping on her course to the pole, all she would have to do would be to turn around and come back. As to the possibility of receiving no messages, I should conclude in that case that the wire had broken, and should wait a few days before allowing myself to be seriously alarmed. We have provided against such an accident. The Dipsey is equipped as a cable-laying vessel, and if her broken wire is not at too great a depth, she could recover it; but I have given orders that should such an accident occur, and they cannot reestablish communication, they must return."

"Where to?" asked Mrs. Raleigh.

"To Cape Tariff, of course. The Dipsey cannot navigate the surface of the ocean for any considerable distance."

"And then?" she asked.

"I would go as quickly as possible to St. John's, where I have arranged that a vessel shall be ready for me, and I would meet the party at Cape Tariff, and there plan for a resumption of the enterprise, or bring them home. If they should not be able to get back to Cape Tariff, then all is blank before me. We must not think of it."

"But you will go up there all the same?" she said.

"Oh yes, I will go there."

Mrs. Raleigh made no answer, but sat looking upon the floor.

Frank R. Stockton

"But why should we trouble ourselves with these fears?" continued Clewe. "We have considered all probable dangers and have provided against them, and at this moment everything is going on admirably, and there is every reason why we should feel hopeful and encouraged. I am sorry to see you look so anxious and downcast."

"Mr. Clewe," said she, "I have many anxieties; that is natural, and I cannot help it, but there is only one fear which seriously affects me."

"And that makes you pale," said Clewe. "Are you afraid that if I begin work with the Artesian ray I shall become so interested in it that I shall forget our friends up there in the North? There is no danger. No matter what I might be doing with the ray, I can disconnect the batteries in an instant, lock up the lens-house, and in the next half-hour start for St. John's. Then I will go North if there is anything needed to be done there which human beings can do."

She looked at him steadfastly.

"That is what I am afraid of," she said.

Roland Clewe did not immediately speak. To him Margaret Raleigh was two persons. She was a woman of business, earnest, thoughtful, helpful, generous, and wise; a woman with whom he worked, consulted, planned, who made it possible for him to carry on the researches and enterprises to which he had devoted his life. But, more than this, she was another being; she was a woman he loved, with a warm, passionate love, which grew day by day, and which a year ago had threatened to break down every barrier of prudence, and throw him upon his knees before her as a humiliated creature who had been pretending to love knowledge, philosophy, and science, but in reality had been loving beauty and riches. It was the fear of this catastrophe which had had a strong influence in taking him to Europe.

But now, by some magical influence—an influence which he was not sure he understood—that first woman, the woman of business, his partner, his co-worker, had disappeared, and there sat before him the woman he loved. He felt in his soul that if he tried to banish her it would be impossible; by no word or act could he at this moment bring back the other.

"Margaret Raleigh," he said, suddenly, "you have thrown me from my balance. Yon may not believe it, you may not be able to imagine the possibility of it, but a spirit, a fiery spirit which I have long kept bound up within me, has burst its bonds and has taken possession of me. It may be a devil or it may be an angel, but it holds me and rules me, and it was set loose by the words you have just spoken. It is my love for you, Margaret Raleigh!" He went on, speaking rapidly. "Now tell me," said he. "I have often come to you for advice and help—give it to me now. In laboratory, workshop, office, with you and away from you, abroad and at home, by day and by night, always and everywhere I have loved you, longed for a sight of you, for a word from you, even if it had been a word about a stick or a pin. And always and everywhere I have determined to be true to myself, true to you, true to every principle of honor and common-sense, and to say nothing to you of love until by some success I have achieved the right to do so. By words which made me fancy that you showed a personal interest in me, you have banished all those resolutions; you have—But I am getting madder and madder. Shall I leave this room? Shall I swear never to speak—"

She looked up at him. The ashiness had gone out of her face. Her eyes were bright, and as she lifted them towards him a golden softness and mistiness came into the centre of each of them, as though he might look down through them into her soul.

"If I were you," said she, "I would stay here and say whatever else you have to say."

He told her what more he had to say, but it was with his arms around her and his eyes close to hers.

"Do you know," she said, a little afterwards, "that for years, while you have been longing to get to the pole, to see down into the earth, and to accomplish all the other wonderful things that you are working at in your shops, I too have been longing to do something—longing hundreds and hundreds of times when we were talking about batteries and lenses and of the enterprises we have had on hand."

"And what was that?" he asked.

"It was to push back this lock of hair from your forehead. There, now; you don't know how much better you look!"

Before Clewe left the house it was decided that if in any case it should become necessary for him to start for the polar regions these two were to be married with all possible promptness, and they were to go to the North together.

That afternoon the happy couple met again and composed a message to the arctic seas. It was not deemed necessary yet to announce to society what had happened, but they both felt that their friends who were so far away, so completely shut out from all relations with the world, and yet so intimately connected with them, should know that Margaret Raleigh and Roland Clewe were engaged to be married.

Roland sent the message that evening from his office. He waited an unusually long time for a reply, but at last it came, from Sammy. The cipher, when translated, ran as follows:

"Everybody as glad as they can be. Specially Sarah. Will

send regular congratulations. Private message soon from me. We have got the devil on board."

Clewe was astonished: Samuel Block was such a quiet, steady person, so unused to extravagance or excitement, that this sensational message was entirely beyond his comprehension. He could fix no possible meaning to it, and he was glad that it did not come when he was in company with Margaret. It was too late to disturb her now, and he most earnestly hoped that an explanation would come before he saw her again.

That night he dreamed that there was a great opening near the pole, which was the approach to the lower regions, and that the Dipsey had been boarded by a diabolical passenger, who had come to examine her papers and inquire into the health of her passengers and crew.

Frank R. Stockton

CHAPTER VIII

THE DEVIL ON THE DIPSEY

After a troubled night, Roland Clewe rose early. He had made up his mind that what Sammy had to communicate was something of a secret, otherwise it would have been telegraphed at once. For this reason he had not sent him a message asking for immediate and full particulars, but had waited. Now, however, he felt he could wait no longer; he must know something definite before he saw Margaret. Not to excite suspicion by telegraphing at untimely hours, he had waited until morning, and as the Dipsey was in about the same longitude as Sardis, and as they kept regular hours on board, without regard to the day and night of the arctic regions, he knew that he would not now be likely to rouse anybody from his slumbers by "calling up" the pole.

Although the telephone had been brought to such wonderful perfection in these days, Roland Clewe had never thought of using it for purposes of communication with the Dipsey. The necessary wire would have been too heavy, and his messages could not have been kept secret. In fact, this telegraphic communication between Sardis and the submarine vessel was almost as primitive as that in use in the latter part of the nineteenth century.

But Clewe had scarcely entered the office when he was

surprised by the sound of the instrument, and he soon found that Sammy was calling to him from the polar seas. He sat down instantly and received this message:

"Could not send more last night. Gibbs came in. Did not want him to know until I had heard from you. That Pole, Rovinski, is on board. Never knew it until yesterday. Had shaved off his beard and had his head cropped. He let it grow, and I spotted him. There is no mistake. I know him, but he has not found it out. He is on board to get ahead of you some way or other —perhaps get up a mutiny and go to the pole himself. He is the wickedest-looking man I ever saw, and he scared me when I first recognized him. Will send news as long as I am on hand. Let me know what you think. I want to chuck him into the scuttle-box.

"SAMUEL BLOCK."

"If that could be done," said Clewe to himself, "it would be an end to a great many troubles."

The scuttle-box on the submarine vessel was a contrivance for throwing things overboard. It consisted of a steel box about six feet long and two feet square at the ends, and with a tightly fitting door at each extremity. When this scuttle-box was used it was run down through a square opening in the bottom of the Dipsey, the upper door was opened, matter to be disposed of was thrown into it, the upper door was shut and the lower one opened, whereupon everything inside of it descended into the sea, and water filled the box. When this box was drawn up by means of its machinery, the water was forced out, so that when it was entirely inside the vessel it was empty, and then the lower door was closed. For some moments the idea suggested by Sammy was very attractive to Clewe, and he could not help thinking that the occasion might arise when it would be perfectly proper to carry it into execution.

Now that he knew the import of Sammy's extraordinary communication, he felt that it would not be right to withhold his knowledge from Margaret. Of course it might frighten her very much, but this was an enterprise in which people should expect to be frightened. Full confidence and hearty assistance were what these two now expected from each other.

"What is it exactly that you fear?" she asked, when she had heard the news.

"That is hard to say," replied Roland. "This man Rovinski is a scientific jackal; he has ambitions of the very highest kind, and he seeks to gratify them by fraud and villainy. It is now nearly two years since I have found out that he has been shadowing me, endeavoring to discover what I am doing and how I am doing it; and the moment he does get a practical and working knowledge of anything, he will go on with the business on my lines as far as he can. Perhaps he may succeed, and, in any case, he will be almost certain to ruin my chances of success—that is, if I were not willing to buy him off. He would be pretty sure to try blackmail if he found he could not make good use of the knowledge he had stolen."

"The wretch!" cried Margaret. "Do you suppose he hopes to snatch from you the discovery of the pole?"

"That seems obvious," replied Roland, "and it's what Sammy thinks. It is the greatest pity in the world he was not discovered before he got on the Dipsey."

"But what can you do?" cried Margaret.

"I cannot imagine," he replied, "unless I recall the Dipsey to Cape Tariff, and go up there and have him apprehended."

"Couldn't he be apprehended where he is?" she asked. "There

are enough men on board to capture him and shut him up somewhere where he could do no harm."

"I have thought of that," answered Roland, "but it would be a very difficult and delicate thing to do. The men we have on board the Dipsey are trusty fellows—at least, I thought so when they were engaged—but there is no knowing what mutinous poison this Pole may have infused into their minds. If one of their number should be handcuffed and shut up without good reason being given, they might naturally rebel, and it would be very hard to give satisfactory reasons for arresting Rovinski. Even Gibbs might object to such harshness upon grounds which might seem to him vague and insufficient. Sammy knows Rovinski, I know him, but the others do not, and it might be difficult to convince them that he is the black-hearted scoundrel we think him; so we must be very careful what we do."

"As to calling the Dipsey back," said Margaret, "I would not do it; I would take the risks."

"I think you are right," said Clewe. "I have a feeling that if they come back to Cape Tariff they will not go out again. Some of the men may be discouraged already, and it would produce a bad impression upon all of them to turn back for some reason which they did not understand, or for a reason such as we could give them. I would not like to have to bring them back, now that they are getting on so well."

In the course of the morning there came from the officers, men, and passenger of the Dipsey a very cordial and pleasant message to Mr. Clewe and Mrs. Raleigh, congratulating them upon the happy event of which they had been informed. Sarah Block insisted on sending a supplementary message for herself, in which she was privately congratulatory to as great an extent as her husband would allow her to go, and which ended with a hope that if they lived to be married they would content themselves with doing their explorations on solid ground. She did not want to come back until she had seen the pole, but some of her ideas about that kind of travelling were getting to be a good deal more fixed than they had been.

The advice which Roland Clewe gave to Samuel Block was simple enough and perhaps unnecessary, but there was noshing else for him to say. He urged that the strictest watch be kept on Rovinski; that he should never be allowed to go near the telegraph instrument; and if, by insubordination or any bad conduct, a pretext for his punishment should offer itself, he should be immediately shut up where he could not communicate with the men. It was very important to keep him as much as possible in ignorance of what was going on and of what should be accomplished; that, after all, was the main point. If the pole should be discovered, Rovinski must have nothing to do with it. Sammy replied that everything should he reported as soon as it turned up, and any orders received from Mr. Clewe should be carried out so long as he was alive to help carry them.

"Now," said Roland to Margaret, "there's nothing more that we can do in regard to that affair. As soon as there are any new developments we shall have to consider it again, but until then let us give up our whole souls to each other and the Artesian ray."

"It seems to me," said she, "that if we could have discovered a good while ago some sort of ray by which we could see into each other's souls, we should have gained a great many hours which are now lost."

"Not at all," replied Clewe; "they are not lost. In our philosophy, nothing is lost. All the joys we have missed in days that are past shall be crowded into the days that are to come."

CHAPTER IX

THE ARTESIAN RAY

In less than a week after the engagement of Roland Clewe and Margaret Raleigh work on the great machine which was to generate the Artesian ray had so far progressed that it was possible to make some preliminary experiments with it. Although Clewe was sorry to think of the very undesirable companion which Samuel Block had carried with him into the polar regions, he could not but feel a certain satisfaction when he reflected that there was now no danger of Rovinski gaining any knowledge of the momentous operations which he had in hand in Sardis. He had had frequent telegrams from Sammy, but no trouble of any kind had yet arisen. It was true that the time for trouble, if there were to be any, had probably not yet arrived, but Clewe could not afford to disturb his mind with anticipations of disagreeable things which might happen.

The masses of lenses, batteries, tubes, and coils which constituted the new instrument had been set up in the lens-house, and it was with this invention that Clewe had succeeded in producing that new form of light which would not only penetrate any material substance, but illuminate and render transparent everything through which it passed, and which would, it was hoped, extend itself into the earth to a depth only limited by the electric power used to generate it.

Margaret was very anxious to be present at the first experiment, but Clewe was not willing that this should be.

"It is almost certain," he said, "that there will be failures at first, not caused perhaps by any radical defects in the apparatus, but by some minor fault in some part of it. This almost always happens in a new machine, and then there are uninteresting work and depressing waiting. As soon as I see that my invention will act as I want it to act, I shall have you in the lens-house with me. We may not be able to do very much at first, but when I really begin to do anything I want both of us to see it done."

There was no flooring in that part of the lens-house where the machine was set up, for Clewe wished his new light to operate directly upon the earth. At about eight feet above the ground was the opening through which the Artesian ray would pass perpendicularly downward whenever the lever should be moved which would connect the main electric current.

When all was ready, Clewe sent every one, even Bryce, the master-workman, from the room. If his invention should totally fail, he wanted no one but himself to witness that failure; but if it should succeed, or even give promise of doing so, he would be glad to have the eyes of his trusted associates witness that success. When the doors were shut and locked, Clewe moved a lever, and a disk of light three feet in diameter immediately appeared upon the ground. It was a colorless light, but it seemed to give a more vivid hue to everything it shone upon—such as the little stones, a piece of wood half embedded in the earth, grains of sand, and pieces of mortar. In a few seconds, however, these things all disappeared, and there revealed itself to the eyes of Clewe a perfectly smooth surface of brown earth. This continued for some little time, now and then a rounded or a flattened stone appearing in it, and then gradually fading away.

As Clewe stared intently down upon the illuminated space, the brown earth seemed to melt and disappear, and he gazed upon a surface of fine sand, dark or yellowish, thickly interspersed with gravel-stones. This appearance changed, and a large rounded stone was seen almost in the centre of the glowing disk. The worn and smooth surface of the stone faded away, and he beheld what looked like a split section of a cobble-stone. Then it disappeared altogether, and there was another flat surface of gravel and sand.

Between himself and the illuminated space on which he gazed—his breath quick and his eyes widely distended—there seemed to be nothing at all. To all appearances he was looking into a cylindrical hole a few feet deep. Everything between the bottom of this hole and himself was invisible; the light had made intervening substances transparent, and had deprived them of color and outlines. It was as though he looked through air.

Then his eyes fell upon the sides of this cylindrical opening, and these, illuminated, but not otherwise acted upon by the volume of Artesian rays, showed, in all their true colors and forms, everything which went to make up the sides of the bright cavity into which he looked. He saw the various strata of clay, sand, gravel, exactly as he would have seen them in a circular hole cut accurately and smoothly into the earth. No stone or lump protruded from the side of this apparent excavation, the inner surface of which was as smooth as if it had been cut down with a sharp instrument.

Clewe was frightened. Was it possible that this could be an imaginary cavity into which he was looking? He drew back; he was about to put out one foot to feel if it were really solid ground upon which this light was pouring, but he refrained. He got a long stick, and with it touched the centre of the light. What he felt was hard and solid; the end of the stick seemed to melt, and this startled him. He pulled back the

Frank R. Stockton

stick—he could go on no further by himself. He must have somebody in here with him; he must have the testimony of some other eyes; he needed the company of a man with a cool and steady brain.

He ran to the door and called Bryce. When the master-workman had entered and the door had been locked behind him, he exclaimed, "How pale you are! Does it work?"

"I think so," said Clewe; "but perhaps I am crazy and only imagine it. You see that circular patch of light upon the ground there? I want you to go close to it and look down upon it, and tell me what you see."

Bryce stepped quickly to the illuminated space. He looked down at it; then he approached nearer; then he carefully placed his feet by its edge and leaned over further, gazing intently downward, and he exclaimed, "Good heavens! How did you make the hole?"

At that moment he heard a groan, and, looking across the illuminated space, he saw Clewe tottering. In the next moment he was stretched upon the ground in a dead faint.

When Bryce had hurried to the side of his employer and had thrown a pitcher of water over him, it was not long before Clewe revived. In answer to Bryce's inquiries he simply replied that he supposed he had been too much excited by the success of his work.

"You see," said he, "that was not a hole at all that you were looking into; it was the solid earth made transparent by the Artesian ray. The thing works perfectly. Please step to that lever and turn it off. I can stand no more at present."

Bryce moved the lever, and the light upon the ground disappeared. He approached the place where it had been; it was nothing but common earth. He put his foot upon it; he stamped; it was as solid as any other part of the State.

"And yet I have looked down into it," he ejaculated, "at least half a dozen feet!"

When Bryce turned and went back to Clewe, he too was pale.

"I do not wonder you fainted," said he. "I do not believe it was what you saw that upset you; it was what you expected to see —wasn't that it?"

Clewe nodded in an indefinite way. "We won't talk about it now," said he. "I don't want any more experiments to-day. We will cover up the instrument and go."

When Roland Clewe reached his room, he sat down in the arm-chair to think. He had made a grand and wonderful success, but it was not upon that that his mind was now fixed. It was upon the casual and accidental effect of the work of his invention, of which he had never dreamed. Bryce had made a great mistake in thinking that it was not what Roland Clewe had seen, but what he had expected to see, which had caused him to drop insensible. It was what he had seen.

When the master-workman had approached the lighted space upon the ground, Clewe stood opposite to him, a little distance from the apparatus. As Bryce looked down, he leaned forward more and more, until the greater part of his body was directly over the lighted space. Looking at him, Clewe was startled, amazed, and horrified to find all that portion of his person which projected itself into the limits of the light had entirely disappeared, and that he was gazing upon a section of a man's trunk, brightly illuminated, and displayed in all its internal colors and outlines. Such a sight was enough to take away the senses of any man, and he did not wonder that he had fainted.

"Now," said he to himself, "all the time that I was looking into that apparent hole, never thinking that in order to see down into it I was obliged to project a portion of myself into the line of the Artesian ray, that portion of me was transparent, invisible. If Bryce had come in! and then"—as the thought came into his mind his heart stopped beating— "if Margaret had been there!"

For an hour he sat in his chair, racking his brain.

"She must see the working of the ray," he said. "I must tell her of my success. She must see it as soon as possible. It is cruel to keep her waiting. But how shall I manage it? How shall I shield her from the slightest possibility of what happened to me? Heavens!" he exclaimed, "if she had been there!"

After a time he determined that before any further experiments should take place he would build a circular screen, a little room, which should entirely surround the space on which the Artesian ray was operated. Only one person at a time should be allowed to enter this screened apartment, which should then be closed. It would make no difference if one should become invisible, provided there was no one else to know it.

It was on the evening of the next day that Margaret beheld the action of the Artesian ray. She greatly objected at first to going inside of the screened space by herself, and urged Roland to accompany her; but this he stoutly refused to do, assuring her that it was essential for but one person at a time to view the action of the ray. She demurred a good deal, but at last consented to allow herself to be shut up within the screen.

What Margaret saw was different from the gradual excavation which had revealed itself before the eyes of Roland. She looked immediately into a hole nearly ten feet deep. The action of the apparatus was such that the power of penetration gained by the ray during its operation at any time was retained, so that when the current was shut off the photic boring ceased, and recommenced when the batteries were again put into action at the point where it had left off. The moment Margaret looked down she gave a little cry, and started back against the screen. She was afraid she would fall in.

"Roland," she exclaimed, "you don't mean to say that this is not really an opening into the earth?"

He was near her on the other side of the screen, and he explained to her the action of the light. Over and over she asked him to come inside and tell her what it was she saw, but he always refused.

"The bottom is beautifully smooth and gray," she exclaimed; "what is that?"

"Sand," said Roland.

"And now it is white, like a piece of pottery," she exclaimed.

"That is white clay," said he.

"Don't you want to take my place," said she, "if you will not come with me?"

"No," said Roland. "Look down as long as you wish; I know pretty well what you will see for some time to come. Has there been any change?"

"The bottom is still white," she replied, "but it is glittering."

"That is white sand," said he. "The Artesian well which supplies the works revealed to me long ago the character of the soil at this spot, so that for a hundred feet or more I know what we may expect to see."

She came out hurriedly. "When you begin to speak of wells," she said, "I am frightened. If I should see water, I should lose my head." She sat down and put her hand before her eyes. "My brain is dazzled," she said. "I don't feel strong enough to believe what I have seen."

Roland shut off the current and opened the screen. "Come here, Margaret," he said; "this is the spot upon which the light was shining. I think it will do you good to look at it. Tread upon it; it will help to reassure you that the things about us are real."

Margaret was silent for a few moments, and then, approaching Roland, she took him by both hands. "You have succeeded," said she; "you are the greatest discoverer of this age!"

"My dear Margaret," he interrupted, quickly, "do not let us talk in that way; we have only just begun to work. Above all things, do not let us get excited. If everything works properly, it will not be long before I can send the Artesian ray down into depths with which I am not acquainted—how far I do not know—but we must wait and see what is the utmost we can do. When we have reached that point, it will be in order to hoist our flags and blow our trumpets. I hope it will not be long before the light descends so deep that we shall be obliged to use a telescope."

"And will it not be possible, Roland," Margaret said, earnestly, "that we shall ever look down into the earth together? When the light gets beyond the depth to which people have dug and bored, I shall never want to stand there alone behind the screen and see what next shall show itself."

"That screen is an awkward affair," said Roland. "Perhaps I may think of a method by which it can be done away with, and by which we can stand side by side and look down as far into the depths of the earth as our Artesian ray can be induced to bore."

Frank R. Stockton

CHAPTER X

"LAKE SHIVER"

Steadily the Dipsey worked her way northward, and as she moved on her course her progress became somewhat slower than it had been at first. This decrease in speed was due partially to extreme caution on the part of Mr. Gibbs, the Master Electrician.

The attenuated cable, which continually stretched itself out behind the little vessel, was of the most recent and improved pattern for deep-sea cables. The conducting wires in the centre of it were scarcely thicker than hairs, while the wires forming the surrounding envelope, although they were so small as to make the whole cable not more than an eighth of an inch in diameter, were far stronger than the thick submarine cables which were used in the early days of ocean telegraphy. These outer wires were made of the Swedish toughened steel fibre, and in 1939, with one of them a little over a sixteenth of an inch in diameter, a freight-ship of eleven thousand tons had been towed through the Great New Jersey Canal, which had then just been opened, and which connected Philadelphia with the ocean.

But notwithstanding his faith in the strength of the cable, Mr. Gibbs felt more and more, the farther he progressed from the habitable world, the importance of preserving it from accident. He had gone so far that it would be a grievous thing to be obliged to turn back.

The Dipsey sailed at a much lower depth than when she had first started upon her submarine way. After they had become accustomed to the feeling of being surrounded by water, her inmates seemed to feel a greater sense of security when they were well down below all possible disturbing influence. When they looked forward in the line of the search-light, or through any of the windows in various parts of the vessel, they never saw anything but water—no fish, nothing floating. They were too far below the ice above them to see it, and too far from what might be on either side of them to catch a glimpse of it. The bottom was deep below them, and it was as though they were moving through an aqueous atmosphere.

They were comfortable, and beginning to be accustomed to their surrounding circumstances. The air came in regularly and steadily through the electric gills, and when deteriorated air had collected in the expiration-chamber in the upper part of the vessel, it was forced out by a great piston, which sent it by a hundred little valves into the surrounding water. Thus the pure air came in and the refuse air went out just as if the little Dipsey had been healthfully breathing as it pushed its way through the depths.

Mrs. Block was gaining flesh. The narrow accommodations, the everlasting electric light, the sameness of food, and a total absence of incident had become quite natural to her, and she had ceased to depend upon the companionship of the dust-brush and the almanac to carry her mind back to what she considered the real things of life.

Sarah had something better now to take her mind back to Sardis and the people and things on dry land. The engagement and probably early marriage of Mr. Clewe and

Mrs. Raleigh had made a great impression upon her, and there were days when she never thought of the pole, so busy was she in making plans based upon the future connection of the life of herself and Sammy and that of Mr. and Mrs. Clewe.

Sammy and his wife had very good quarters within the boundaries of the works, but Sarah had never been quite satisfied with them, and when the new household of Clewe should be set up, and all the new domestic arrangements should be made, she hoped for better things. Mr. Clewe's little cottage would then be vacant, for of course he and his wife would not live in such a place as that, and she thought that she and Sammy should have it. Hour by hour and day by day she planned the furnishing, the fitting, and the management of this cottage.

She was determined to have a servant, a woman thoroughly capable of doing general house-work; and then there were times when she believed that if Sammy should succeed in finding the pole his salary would be increased, and they might be able to afford two servants. Over and over again did she consider the question whether, in this latter case, these women should both be general house-work servants, or one of them a cook and the other a chamber-maid and laundress. There was much to be considered on each side. In the latter case more efficient work could be obtained; but in the former, in case one of them should suddenly leave, or go away for a day out, the other could do all the work. It was very pleasant to Mrs. Block to sit in a comfortable arm-chair and gaze thus into the future. Sometimes she looked up into the water above, and sometimes out into the water ahead, but she could see nothing. But in the alluring expanse of her fancied future she could see anything which she chose to put there.

Sammy, however, did not increase in flesh; in fact, he grew

thinner. Nothing important in regard to the Pole, Rovinski, had occurred, but of course something would occur; otherwise why did the Pole come on board the Dipsey? Endless conjectures as to what Rovinski would do when he did anything, and when he would begin to do it, kept the good Samuel awake during many hours when he should have been soundly sleeping. He had said nothing yet to Mr. Gibbs in regard to the matter. Every day he made a report to Roland Clewe about Rovinski, but Clewe's instructions were that so long as the Pole behaved himself properly there was no reason to trouble the minds of the party on board with fears of rascality on his part. They had enough to occupy their minds without any disturbing influence of that sort.

Clewe's own opinion on the subject was that Rovinski could do nothing but act as a spy, and afterwards make dishonest use of the knowledge he should acquire; but the man had put himself into Clewe's power, and he could not possibly get away from him until he should return to Cape Tariff, and even there it would be difficult. The proper and only thing to do was to keep him in custody as long as possible. When he should be brought back to a region of law and justice, it might be that the Pole could be prevented, for a time, at least, from using the results of his knavish observations.

There was another person on board whose mind was disturbed by Rovinski. This was Mr. Marcy, the Assistant Engineer, an active, energetic fellow, filled with ambition and love of adventure, and one of the most hopeful and cheerful persons on board. He had never heard of Rovinski, and did not know that there was anybody in the world who was trying to benefit himself by fraudulent knowledge of Mr. Clewe's discoveries and inventions, but he hated the Pole on his own account.

The man's countenance was so villainous that it was enough of itself to arouse the dislike of a healthy-minded young fellow such as Marcy; but, moreover, the Pole had habits of sneaking about the vessel, and afterwards retiring to quiet corners, where he would scribble in a pocket notebook. Such conduct as this in a man whose position corresponded with that of a common seaman on an ordinary vessel, seemed contrary to discipline and good conduct, and he mentioned the matter to Mr. Gibbs.

"I suppose the man is writing a letter to his wife," said the latter. "You would not want to hinder him from doing that, would you?"

And to this no good answer could be made.

The Pole never took notes when Sammy was anywhere where he could see him, and if Mr. Marcy had reported this conduct to the old man, it is likely that Rovinski would speedily have been deprived of pencils and paper, and his real character made known to the officers.

One day it was observed by those who looked out of the window in the upper deck that the water above them was clearer than they usually saw it, and when the electric lights in the room immediately under the window were turned out it was almost possible to discern objects in the room. Instantly there was a great stir on board the Dipsey, and observations soon disclosed the fact that there was nothing above the vessel but water and air.

At first, like an electric flash, the thought ran through the vessel that they had reached the open sea which is supposed to surround the pole, but reflection soon showed those who were cool enough to reflect that if this were the case that sea must be much larger than they had supposed, for they were still a long way from the pole. Upon one thing, however, everybody was agreed: they must ascend without loss of time to the surface of the water above them.

Up went the Dipsey, and it was not long before the great glass in the upper deck admitted pure light from the outer world. Then the vessel rose boldly and floated upon the surface of the open sea.

The hatchways were thrown open, and in a few moments nearly everybody on board stood upon the upper deck, breathing the outer air and gazing about them in the pure sunlight. The deck was almost flat, and surrounded by a rail. The flooring was wet, and somewhat slippery, but nobody thought of that; they thought of nothing but the wonderful place in which they found themselves.

They were in a small lake surrounded by lofty and precipitous icebergs. On every side these glittering crags rose high into the air; nowhere was there a break or an opening. They seemed to be in a great icy prison. It might be supposed that it would be exhilarating to a party who had long been submerged beneath the sea to stand once more in the open air and in the light of day; but this was not the case. The air they breathed was sharp and cold, and cut into throats and lungs now accustomed to the softer air within their vessel. Scarcely any of them, hurrying out of the warm cabins, had thought of the necessity of heavy wraps, and the bitter cold of the outer air perceptibly chilled their blood. Involuntarily, even while they were staring about them, they hurried up and down the deck to keep themselves warm.

The officers puzzled their brains over the peculiar formation of this ice-encompassed lake. It seemed as if a great ice mountain had sunk down from the midst of its companions, and had left this awful hole. This, however, was impossible. No law of nature would account for such a disappearance of an ice mountain. Mr. Gibbs thought, under some peculiar circumstances, a mass of ice might have broken away and floated from its surroundings, and that afterwards, increased in size, it had floated back again, and, too large to re-enter the opening it had made, had closed up the frozen walls of this lonely lake, accessible only to those who should rise up into it from the sea. Suddenly Mrs. Block stopped.

"What is that?" she cried, pointing to a spot in the icy wall which was nearest to the vessel. Instantly every eye was turned that way. They saw a very distinct, irregular blotch, surrounded by almost transparent ice.

Several glasses were now levelled upon this spot, and it was discovered to be the body of a polar bear, lying naturally upon its side, as if asleep, and entirely incased in ice.

"It must have lain down to die, on the surface of the ice," said Mr. Gibbs, "and gradually the ice has formed above it, until it now rests in that vast funeral casket."

"How long since he laid down there to die, Mr. Gibbs?" asked Sarah, as she took the glass from her eye. "He looks as natural as if he was asleep."

"I cannot say," he answered. "It may have been hundreds, even thousands, of years ago."

"Oh, horrible!" said Sarah. "All that makes me shiver, and I am sure I don't need anything to make me do that. I wish we would go down, Sammy; I would like to get out of this awful place, with those dreadful glitterin' walls that nobody could get up or over, and things lyin' frozen for a thousand years; and, besides, it's so cold!"

It seemed as if Sarah's words had struck the key-note to the feelings of the whole company. In the heart of every one arose a strong desire to sink out of this cold, bleak, terrifying open air into the comfortable motherly arms of the encircling waters. For a few minutes Captain Jim Hubbell had experienced a sense of satisfaction at finding himself once more upon the deck of a vessel floating upon the open sea. He felt that he was in his element, and that the time had come for him to assume his proper position as a sailor; but this feeling soon passed, and he declared that his spine was like a long icicle.

"Don't you think we had better go down again?" said Sammy. "I think we have all seen enough of this, and it isn't anything that any use can be made of."

"You are right," said Mr. Gibbs; "let everybody go below."

But it was not easy for everybody to obey this command. The wet decks were now covered with a thin surface of ice, and those who had been standing still for a few moments found it difficult to release their shoes from the flooring of the deck, while several of the men slipped down as they made their way to the forward hatch. As for Sarah Block, she found it impossible to move at all. Her shoes were of a peculiar kind, the soles being formed of thick felt, and these, having been soaked with water, had frozen firmly to the deck. She tried to make a step and almost fell over.

"Heavens and earth!" she screamed; "don't let this boat go down and leave me standing outside!"

Her husband and two men tried to release her, but they could not disengage her shoes from the deck; so Sammy was obliged to loosen her shoe-strings, and then he and another man lifted her out of her shoes and carried her to the hatchway, whence she very speedily hurried below.

Everybody was now inside the vessel, the hatches were tightly closed, and the Dipsey began to sink. When she had descended to the comparatively temperate depths of the sea, and her people found themselves in her warm and well-lighted compartments, there was a general disposition to go about and shake hands with each other. Some of them even sang little snatches of songs, so relieved were they to get down out of that horrible upper air.

"Of course I shall never see my shoes again," said Mrs. Block; "and they were mighty comfortable ones, too. I suppose, when they have been down here awhile in this water, which must be almost lukewarmish compared to what it is on top, they will melt loose and float up; and then, Sammy, suppose they lodge on some of that ice and get frozen for a thousand years! Good gracious! It sets me all of a creep to think of that happenin' to my shoes, that I have been wearin' every day! Don't you want a cup of tea?"

"It's a great pity," thought Sammy to himself, "that it wasn't that Pole that had his feet frozen to the deck. The rest of us might have been lucky enough not to have noticed him as the boat went down."

"We ought to get a name for that body of water up there," said Mr. Gibbs, as he was writing out his report of the day's adventures. "Shall we call it 'Lake Clewe'?"

"Oh, don't do that!" exclaimed Sammy Block. "Mr. Clewe's too good a man to have his name tacked on to that hole. If you want to name it, why don't you call it 'Lake Shiver'?"

"That is a good name," answered Mr. Gibbs; and so it was called.

CHAPTER XI

THEY BELIEVE IT IS THE POLAR SEA

With no intention of ascending again into any accidental holes in the ice above them, the voyagers on the Dipsey kept on their uneventful way, until, upon the third day after their discovery of the lake, the electric bell attached to the heavy lead which always hung suspended below the vessel, rang violently, indicating that it had touched the bottom. This sound startled everybody on board. In all their submarine experiences they had not yet sunk down low enough to be anywhere near the bottom of the sea.

Of course orders were given to ascend immediately, and at the same time a minor search-light was directed upward through the deck skylight. To the horror of the observers, ice could plainly be seen stretching above them like an irregular, gray sky.

Here was a condition of things which had not been anticipated. The bottom below and the ice above were approaching each other. Of course it might have been some promontory of the rocks under the sea against which their telltale lead had struck; but there was an instrument on board for taking soundings by means of a lead suspended outside and a wire running through a water-proof hole in the bottom of the vessel, and when the Dipsey had risen a few fathoms, and was progressing very slowly, this instrument was used at frequent intervals, and it was found that the electric lead had not touched a rock projecting upward, and that the bottom was almost level.

Mr. Gibbs's instrument gave him an approximate idea of the vessel's depth in the water, and the dial connected with the sounding apparatus told him hour by hour that the distance from the bottom, as the vessel kept forward on the same plane, was becoming less and less. Consequently he determined, so long as he was able to proceed, to keep the Dipsey as near as possible at a median distance between the ice and the bottom.

This was an anxious time. So long as they had felt that they had plenty of sea-room the little party of adventurers had not yet recognized any danger which they thought sufficient to deter them from farther progress; but if the ice and the bottom were coming together, what could they do? It was possible, by means of explosives they carried, to shatter the ice above them; but action of this kind had not been contemplated unless they should find themselves at the pole and still shut in by ice. They did not wish to get out into the open air at the point where they found themselves; and, moreover, it would not have been safe to explode their great bombs in such shallow water. A consultation was held, and it was agreed that the best thing to do was to diverge from the course they had steadily maintained, and try to find a deeper channel leading to the north. Accordingly they steered eastward.

It was not long before they found that they had judged wisely; the bottom descended far out of the reach of their electric lead, and they were enabled to keep a safe distance below the overhanging ice.

"I feel sure," said Mr. Gibbs, "that we came near running

against some outreaching portion of the main Western Continent, and now we have got to look out for the foundations of Greenland's icy mountains." He spoke cheerily, for he wished to encourage his companions, but there was a very anxious look upon his face when he was not speaking to any one.

The next day every one was anxious, whether he spoke or was silent. The bottom was rising again, and the Dipsey was obliged to sail nearer and nearer to the ice above. Between two dangers, constricted and trammelled as they were, none of them could help feeling the terrors of their position, and if it had not been for the encouraging messages which continually came to them from Sardis, they might not have been able to keep up brave hearts.

After two days of most cautious progress, during which the water became steadily shallower and shallower, it was discovered that the ice above, which they were now obliged to approach much more closely than they had ever done before, was comparatively thin, and broken in many places. Great cracks could be seen in it here and there, and movements could be discerned indicating that it was a floe, or floating mass of ice. If that were the case, it was not impossible that they were now nearing the edge of the ice under which they had so long been sailing, and that beyond them was the open water. If they could reach that, and find it the unobstructed sea which was supposed to exist at this end of the earth's axis, their expedition was a success. At that moment they were less than one hundred miles from the pole.

Whether the voyagers on the Dipsey were more excited when the probable condition of their situation became known to them, or whether Roland Clewe and Margaret Raleigh in the office of the Works at Sardis were the more greatly moved when they received that day's report from the arctic regions, it would be hard to say. If there should be room enough for the little submarine vessel to safely navigate beneath the ice which there was such good reason to believe was floating on the edge of the body of water they had come in search of, and on whose surface they might freely sail, what then was likely to hinder them from reaching the pole? The presence of ice in the vicinity of that extreme northern point was feared by no one concerned in the expedition, for it was believed that the rotary motion of the earth would have a tendency to drive it away from the pole by centrifugal force.

The little thermometer-boat which during the submarine voyage of the Dipsey had constantly preceded her to give warning of the sunken base of some great iceberg, was now drawn in close to the bow; there was so much ice so near that its warnings were constant, and therefore unneeded.

The electric lead-line was shortened to the length of a few fathoms, and even then it sometimes suddenly rang out its alarm. After a time the bottom of the sea became visible through the stout glass of a protected window near the bow, and a man was placed there to report what he could see below them.

It had now become so light that in some parts of the vessel the electric lamps were turned out. Fissures of considerable size appeared in the ice above, and then, to the great excitement of every one, the vessel slowly moved under a wide space of open water; but the ice could be seen ahead, and she did not rise. The bottom came no nearer, and the Dipsey moved cautiously on. Nobody thought of eating; they did not talk much, but at every one of the outlooks there were eager faces.

At last they saw nothing above them but floating fragments of ice. Still they kept on, until they were plainly moving below the surface of open water. Then Mr. Gibbs looked at Sammy.

"I think it is time to rise," said he; and Sammy passed the word that the Dipsey was going up into the upper air.

When the little craft, so long submerged in the quiet depths of the Arctic Sea, had risen until she rested on the surface of the water, there was no general desire, as there had been when she emerged into Lake Shiver, to rush upon the upper deck. Instead of that, the occupants gathered together and looked at each other in a hesitating way, as if they were afraid to go out and see whether they were really in an open sea, or lying in some small ice-locked body of water.

Mr. Gibbs was very pale.

"My friends," said he, "we are going on deck to find out whether or not we have reached the open polar sea, but we must not be excited, and we must not jump to hurried conclusions; we may have found what we are in search of, and we may not have found it yet. But we will go up and look out upon the polar world as far as we can see it, and we shall not decide upon this thing or that until we have thoroughly studied the whole situation. The engines are stopped, and every one may go up, but I advise you all to put on your warmest clothes. We should remember our experience at Lake Shiver."

"It wouldn't be a bad idea," said Sammy Block, "to throw out a lot of tarpaulins to stand on, so that none of us will get frozen to the wet deck, as happened before."

When the hatch was opened a man with a black beard pushed himself forward towards the companionway.

"Keep back here, sir," said Mr. Marcy, clapping his hand

upon the man's shoulder.

"I want to be ready to spread the tarpaulins, sir," said he, with a wriggling motion, as if he would free himself.

"You want to be the first to see the polar sea, that is my opinion," said Mr. Marcy; "but you keep back there where you belong." And with that he gave the eager Rovinski a staggering push to the rear.

Five minutes afterwards Margaret Raleigh and Roland Clewe, sitting close together by the telegraph instrument in the Works at Sardis, received the following message:

"We have risen to the surface of what we believe to be the open polar sea. Everybody is on deck but me. It is very cold, and a wind is blowing. Off to our left there are high mountains, stretching westward as far as we can see. They are all snow and ice, but they look blue and green and beautiful. From these mountains there comes this way a long cape, with a little mountain at the end of it. Mr. Gibbs says this mountain, which is about twenty miles away, must be just about between us and the pole, but it does not cut us off. Far out to the right, as far as we can see, there is open water shining in the sun, so that we can sail around the cape. On the right and behind us, southward, are everlasting plains of snow and ice, which we have just come from under. They are so white that it dazzles our eyes to look at them. In some places they are smooth, and in some places they are tumbled up. On the very edge of the sky, in that direction, there are more mountains. There are no animals or people anywhere. It is very cold, even inside the vessel. My fingers are stiff. Now that we are out on the water, in regular shipshape, Captain Jim Hubbell has taken command. We are going to cruise northward as soon as we can get things regulated for outside sailing.

"SAMUEL BLOCK."

CHAPTER XII

CAPTAIN HUBBELL TAKES COMMAND

It was a high-spirited and joyous party that the Dipsey now carried; not one of them doubted that they had emerged from under the ice into the polar sea. To the northeast they could see its waves shining and glistening all the way to the horizon, and they believed that beyond the cape in front of them these waters shone and glistened to the very north. They breathed the polar air, which, as they became used to it, was exhilarating and enlivening, and they basked in the sunshine, which, although it did not warm their bodies very much, cheered and brightened their souls. But what made them happier than anything else was the thought that they would soon start direct for the pole, on top of the water, and with nothing in the way.

When Captain Jim Hubbell took command of the Dipsey the state of affairs on that vessel underwent a great change. He was sharp, exact, and severe; he appreciated the dignity of his position, and he wished to let everybody see that he did so. The men on board who had previously been workmen now became sailors—at least in the eyes of Captain Hubbell. He did not know much about the work that they had been in the habit of doing, but he intended to teach them the duties of sailors just as soon as he could find any such duties for them to perform. He walked about the deck with an important air,

Frank R. Stockton

and looked for something about which he might give orders. There were no masts or spars or shrouds or sheets, but there were tarpaulins on the deck, and these were soon arranged in seamanlike fashion. A compass was rigged up on deck, and Captain Hubbell put himself into communication with the electric steersman.

It was morning when the Dipsey emerged from the sea, although day and night were equally bright at that season, and at twelve o'clock Captain Hubbell took an observation, assisted by Sammy. The result was as follows: longitude, 69 30'; latitude, 88 42'.

"It strikes me," said Captain James Hubbell, "that that latitude goes over anything ever set down by any skipper, ancient or modern."

"I should say so," answered Sammy. "But that record won't be anything compared to what we are goin' to set down."

Work went on very rapidly, in order to get the Dipsey into regular nautical condition, and although it was out of his line, Captain Hubbell made it a point to direct as much of it as he could. The electric gills were packed as close to the side of the vessel as possible, and the various contrivances for heating and ventilation when sailing in the open air were put into working order. At four o'clock in the afternoon our party started to round the icy promontory ahead of them, encouraged by a most hearty and soul-inspiring message from the hills of New Jersey.

"It's all very fine," said Sarah Block to her husband, "for everybody on board to be talkin' about what a splendid thing it is to be sailin' on the surface of the sea, in the bright and beautiful air, but I must say that I like a ship to keep quiet when I am on board of her. I had a pretty bad time when I was comin' up on the Go Lightly, but she was big and didn't wabble like this little thing. We went along beautifully when we were under the water, with the floor just as level as if we were at home, in a house, and now I am not feelin' anything like as well as I have been. For my part, I think it would be a great deal better to sink down again and go the rest of the way under the water. I am sure we found it very comfortable, and a great deal warmer."

Sammy laughed.

"Oh, that would not do at all," he said. "You can't expect the people on board this vessel to be willin' to scoop along under the water when they have got a chance of sailin' like Christians in the open air. It's the sudden change that troubles you, Sarah; you'll soon get over it."

But Sarah was not satisfied. The Dipsey rolled a good deal, and the good woman was frequently obliged to stop and steady herself when crossing the little cabin.

"I feel," said she, "as if I had had a Christmas dinner yesterday and somebody else had made the pies."

The dissatisfied condition of Mrs. Block had a cheering influence upon Captain Hubbell when he heard of it.

"By George!" said he, "this seems like good old times. When I was young and there was women on board, they all got a little sea-sick; but nowadays, with these ball-and-socket ships, you never hear of that sort of thing. A sea-sick woman is the most natural thing I have struck yet on this cruise."

Mrs. Block's uneasiness, however, did not last very long. A few electric capsules of half an alterative volt each soon relieved her; but her mind was still out of order; she was not satisfied. She had accustomed herself to submerged conditions, and ordinary voyaging was very different.

"It wouldn't surprise me," she said, "if we should find that there wasn't any pole; that's about the way these things generally turn out."

In a few hours the Dipsey had rounded the cape, keeping well off shore. In front was a clear sweep of unobstructed water. With their telescopes they could see nothing on the horizon which indicated the presence of land. If the sea should stretch out before them, as they hoped and expected, a sail of about seventy miles ought to bring them to the pole. The Dipsey did not go at full speed; there was no hurry, and as he was in absolutely unknown waters, Captain Hubbell wished to take no risks of sunken reefs or barely submerged islands. Soundings were frequent, and they found that the polar sea—at least that part over which they were sailingwas a comparatively shallow body of water.

Before they left Sardis, preparations had been made for an appropriate and permanent designation of the exact position of the northern end of the earth's axis. If this should be discovered to be on solid land, there was a great iron standard, or column, on board, in detached parts, with all appliances for setting it up firmly in the rocks or earth or ice; but if the end of the said axis should be found to be covered by water of not too great depth, a buoy had been provided which should be anchored upon the polar point.

This buoy was a large hollow, aluminium globe, from which a tall steel flag-post projected upward to a considerable height, bearing a light weather-vane, which, when the buoy should be in its intended position, would always point southward, no matter which way the wind might blow. This great buoy contained various appropriate articles, which had been hermetically sealed up in it before it left Sardis, where it was manufactured. All the documents, books, coins, and other articles which are usually placed in the corner-stones of important buildings were put in this, together with the names of the persons who had gone on this perilous expedition and those who had been its projectors and promoters. More than this, there was an appropriate inscription deeply cut into the metal on the upper part of the buoy, with a space left for the date of the discovery, should it ever take place.

But the mere ceremony of anchoring a buoy at the exact position of the pole was not enough to satisfy the conscientious ambition of Mr. Gibbs. He had come upon this perilous voyage with the earnest intention of doing his duty in all respects, while endeavoring to make the great discovery of the age; and if that discovery should be made, he believed that his country should share in the glory and in the material advantage, whatever that might be, of the achievement. Consequently it was his opinion that if the pole should be discovered, the discoverers should take possession of it in the name of their country. Every one on board—except Sarah Block, who had something to say about the old proverb concerning the counting of chickens before they are hatched—thought this a good idea, and when the plan was submitted to Mr. Clewe and Mrs. Raleigh, they heartily approved.

Preparations were now made to take possession of the pole if they should reach it on the water. On the after-part of the deck a ring about three feet in diameter was marked, and it was arranged that when they had ascertained, by the most accurate observations and calculations, the exact position of the pole, they would so guide their vessel that this ring should be as nearly as possible directly over it. Then one of the party should step inside of the ring and take possession of the pole. After this the buoy would be anchored, and their intended scientific observations and explorations would proceed.

It was supposed both on the Dipsey and at Sardis that Mr. Gibbs would assume the honor of this act of taking

Frank R. Stockton

possession, but that gentleman declined to do so. He considered that he would no more discover the pole, if they should reach it, than would his companions; and he also believed that, from a broad point of view, Mr. Roland Clewe was the real discoverer. Consequently he considered that the direct representative of the interests of Mr. Clewe should take possession, and it was decided that Samuel Block should add the north pole to the territory of his native land.

When this had been settled, a very great change came over the mind of Sarah Block. That her husband should be the man to do this great thing filled her with pride and alert enthusiasm.

"Sammy," she exclaimed, "when you are doin' that, you will be the greatest man in this world, and you will stand at the top of everything."

"Suppose there should be a feller standin' on the south pole," said Sammy, "wouldn't he have the same right to say that he was on top of everything?"

"No," said Sarah, sharply. "The way I look at it, the north pole is above and the south pole is below; but there ain't any other feller down there, so we needn't talk about it. And now, Sammy, if you are goin' to take possession of the pole, you ought to put on your best clothes. For one thing, you should wear a pair of those new red flannel socks that you haven't had on yet; it will be a good way to christen 'em. Everything on you ought to be perfectly fresh and clean, and just as nice as you've got. This will be the first time that anybody ever took possession of a pole, and you ought to look your very best. I would ask you to shave, because you would look better that way, but I suppose if you took off your beard you would take cold in your jaws. And I want you to stand up straight, and talk as long about it as you can. You are too much given to cuttin' off ceremonies mighty short, as I remember was the case when you were statin' your 'pinions about our weddin'; but I had my way then, and I want to have it now. You are goin' to be a big man, Sammy, and your name will go all over the world, so you must screw yourself up to as much eminence as you think you can stand."

Sammy laughed. "Well, I will do what I can," said he; "that is, providin' our chickens are hatched."

"Oh, they'll come out all right," said Sarah. "I haven't the least doubt of it, now that you are to be the chief figure in the hatchin'."

Shortly after the ordinary hour for rising, an order was issued by Captain Hubbell, and enforced by Samuel Block, that no one should be allowed to come on deck who had not eaten breakfast. There were those on board that vessel who would have stayed on deck during all the hours which should have been devoted to sleeping, had it not been so cold. There would probably be nothing to see when they reached the pole, but they wanted to be on hand, that they might see for themselves that there was nothing to see.

CHAPTER XIII

LONGITUDE EVERYTHING

The sun was as high in the polar heavens as it ever rises in that part of the world. Captain Hubbell stood on the deck of the Dipsey. with his quadrant in hand to take an observation. The engines had been stopped, and nearly everybody on the vessel now surrounded him.

"Longitude everything," said Captain James Hubbell, "latitude ninety, which is as near as I can make it out."

"My friends," said Mr. Gibbs, looking about him, "we have found the pole."

And at these words every head was uncovered.

For some moments no one spoke; but there was a look upon the faces of most of the party which expressed a feeling which was voiced by Sarah Block.

"And yet," said she, speaking in a low tone, "there's nothing to see, after all!"

Captain Hubbell's observations and calculations, although accurate enough for all ordinary nautical purposes, were not sufficiently precise to satisfy the demands of the present occasion, and Mr. Gibbs and the electricians began a series of experiments to determine the exact position of the true pole.

The vessel was now steered this way and that, sometimes backed, and then sent forward again. After about an hour of this zigzag work Mr. Gibbs ordered the engine stopped.

"Now," said he, "the ring on the deck is exactly over the pole, and we may prepare to take possession."

At these words Samuel Block disappeared below, followed by his wife.

"That was an odd expression of yours, Captain Hubbell," said Mr. Gibbs, "when you said we had reached longitude everything. It is correct, of course, but it had not struck me in that light."

"Of course it is correct," said Captain Hubbell. "The end of every line of longitude is right here in a bunch. If you were a bird, you could choose one of 'em and fly down along it to Washington or Greenwich or any other point you pleased. Longitude everything is what it is; we've got the whole of 'em right under us."

Now Samuel Block came on deck, where everybody else on board soon gathered. With a furled flag in his hand, dressed in his best and cleanest clothes, and with a large fur cloak thrown over his shoulders, Mr Block advanced towards the ring on the deck, near the compass.

But he was yet several yards from this point when a black figure, crouching close to the deck, issued from among the men, a little in the rear of the party, and made a dash towards the ring. It was the Pole, Rovinski, who had been standing quivering with excitement, waiting for this supreme moment.

Frank R. Stockton

But almost at the same instant there sprang from the side of Mr. Gibbs another figure, with a face livid with agitation. This was Mr. Marcy, who had noticed the foreigner's excitement and had been watching him. Like a stone from a catapult, Mr. Marcy rushed towards Rovinski, taking a course diagonal to that of the latter, and, striking him with tremendous force just before he reached the ring, he threw him against the rail with such violence that the momentum given to his head and body carried them completely over it, and his legs following, the man went headlong into the sea.

Instantly there was a shout of horror. Sarah Block screamed violently, and her husband exclaimed: "That infernal Pole! He has gone down to the pole, and I hope he may stay there!"

"What does all this mean, Mr. Marcy?" roared Captain Hubbell; "and why did you throw him overboard?"

"Never mind now," cried Sammy, his voice rising above the confusion. "I will tell you all about it. I see what he was up to. He wanted to take possession of the pole in his own beastly name, most likely."

"I don't understand a word of all this," exclaimed Mr. Gibbs. "But there is the man; he has risen to the surface."

"Shall we let him sink," cried Sammy, "or haul him aboard?"

"Let the man sink!" yelled Captain Hubbell. "What do you mean, sir?"

"Well, I suppose it wouldn't do," said Sammy, "and we must get him aboard."

Captain Hubbell roared out orders to throw out life-preservers and lower a boat; but, remembering that he was not on board a vessel of the olden times, he changed the order and commanded that a patent boat-hook be used upon the man in the water.

The end of this boat-hook, which could be shot out like a fishing-rod, was hooked into Rovinski's clothes, and he was pulled to the vessel. Then a rope was lowered, and he was hauled on board, shivering and shaking.

"Take him below and put him in irons," cried Sammy.

"Mr. Block," said Captain Hubbell, "I want you to understand that I am skipper of this vessel, and that I am to give orders. I don't know anything about this man; but do you want him put in irons?"

"I do," said Sammy, "for the present."

"Take that man below and put him in irons!" roared Captain Hubbell.

"And give him some dry clothes," added Sarah Block.

When the confusion consequent upon the incident had subsided there was a general desire not to delay for a moment the actual act of taking legal possession of the pole they had discovered.

Sammy now advanced, his fur cap in one hand and his flag in the other, and took his position in the centre of the circle. For a few moments he did not speak, but turned slowly around, as if desirous of availing himself of the hitherto unknown privilege of looking southward in every direction.

"I'm glad he remembers what I told him," said Sarah. "He's making it last as long as he can."

Frank R. Stockton

"As the representative of Roland Clewe, Esq.," said Samuel, deliberately and distinctly, "I take possession of the north pole of this earth in the name of United North America." With these words he unfurled his flag, with its broad red and white stripes, and its seven great stars in the field of blue, and stuck the sharp end of the flagstaff into the deck in the centre of the circle.*

[* It must be understood that at this time the seven great countries of North America—Greenland, Norland (formerly British America, British Columbia, and Alaska), Canada, the United States, Mexico, Central America, and West Indies—were united under one confederated government, and had one flag, a modification of the banner of the dominant nation.]

"Now," said he to his companions, "this pole is ours, and if anybody ever comes into this sea from Russia, or Iceland, or any other place, they will find the north pole has been pre-empted." At this three hearty cheers were given by the assembled company, who thereupon put on their hats.

The rest of that day and part of the next were spent in taking soundings, and very curious and surprising results were obtained. The electric lead, which rang the instant it touched bottom, showed that the sea immediately over the pole was comparatively shallow, while in every direction from this point the depth increased rapidly. Many interesting experiments were made, which determined the character of the bottom and the varied deposits thereupon, but the most important result of the work of Mr. Gibbs and his associates was the discovery of the formation of the extreme northern portion of the earth. The rock-bed of the sea was found to be of the shape of a flattened cone, regularly sloping off from the polar point.

This peculiar form of the solid portion of the earth at the pole was occasioned, Mr. Gibbs believed, by the rotary motion of the bottom of the sea, which moved much more rapidly than the water above it, thus gradually wearing itself away, and giving to our earth that depression at the poles which has been so long known to geographers.

Day after day the experiments went on; but Mr. Gibbs and his associates were extremely interested in what they were doing; some of the rest of the party began to get a little tired of the monotony. There was absolutely nothing to see except water and sky; and although the temperature was frequently some degrees above freezing, and became sometimes quite pleasant as they gradually grew accustomed to the outer arctic atmosphere, those who had no particular occupation to divert their minds made frequent complaints of the cold. There were occasional snow-storms, but these did not last long, and as a rule the skies were clear.

"But think, Sarah," said Samuel Block, in answer to some of her complaints, "what it would be if this were winter, and, instead of being light all the time, it was dark, with the mercury 'way down at the bottom of the thermometer!"

"I don't intend to think of it at all," replied Sarah, sharply. "Do you suppose I am goin' to consent to stay here until the everlastin' night comes on? If that happened, I would simply stretch myself out and die. It's bad enough as it is; but when I look out on the sun, and think that it is the same sun that is shinin' on Sardis, and on the house which I hope we are goin' to have when we get back, I feel as if there was somethin' up here besides you, Sammy, that I'm accustomed to. If it was not for you and the sun, I could not get along at all; but if the sun's gone, I don't think you will be enough. I wish they would plant that corner-stone buoy and let us be off."

But by far the most dissatisfied person on board was the Pole, Rovinski. He was chained to the floor in the hold, and

Frank R. Stockton

could see nothing; nor could he find out anything. Sammy had explained his character and probable intentions to Captain Hubbell, who had thereupon delivered to Mr. Block a very severe lecture for not telling him before.

"If I've got a scoundrel on board I want to know it, and I hope this sort of thing won't happen again, Mr. Block."

"I don't see how it can," answered Sammy; "and I must admit I ought to have told you as soon as you took command; but people don't always do all they ought to do; and, as for tellin' Mr. Gibbs, I would not do that, for his mind is rigged on a hair-spring balance anyway; it wouldn't do to upset him."

"And what are we goin' to do with the feller?" said the captain. "Now that I know what this Pole is, I wish I had let him go down to the other pole and stay there."

"I thought so at first," said Sammy; "but I'm glad he didn't; I'd hate to think of our glorious pole with that thing floppin' on it."

At last all was ready to anchor the great buoy, and preparations were in progress for this important event, when everybody was startled by a shout from Mr. Marcy.

"Hello!" he cried. "What's that? A sail?"

"Where away?" shouted the captain.

"To the south," replied Mr. Marcy. And instantly everybody was looking in opposite directions. But Mr. Marcy's outstretched arm soon indicated to all the position of the cause of his outcry. It was a black spot clearly visible upon the surface of the sea, and apparently about two miles away. Quickly Captain Hubbell had his glass directed upon it, and the next moment he gave a loud cry.

"It's a whale!" he shouted. "There's whales in this polar sea!"

"I thought you said whales were extinct," cried Sammy.

"So I did," replied the captain. "And so they are in all Christian waters. Who ever could have imagined that we would have found 'em here?"

Sarah Block was so frightened when she found there was a whale in the same water in which the Dipsey floated that she immediately hurried below, with an indistinct idea of putting on her things. In such a case as this, it was time for her to leave. But soon recognizing the state of affairs, she sat down in a chair, threw a shawl over her head, and waited for the awful bump.

"Fortunately whales are soft," she said to her, self over and over again.

No one now thought of buoys. Every eye on deck was fixed upon the exposed back of the whale, and everybody speedily agreed that it was coming nearer to them. It did come nearer and nearer, and at one time it raised its head as if it were endeavoring to look over the water at the strange object which had come into those seas. Then suddenly it tossed its tail high into the air and sank out of sight.

"It's a right-whale!" cried Captain Hubbell. "There's whales in this sea! Let's get through this buoy business and go cruisin' after 'em."

There was a great deal of excited talk about the appearance of the whale, but this was not allowed to interfere with the business in hand. A chain, not very heavy but of enormous strength, and of sufficient length to reach the bottom and give plenty of play, was attached to an anchor of a peculiar kind. It was very large and heavy, made of iron, and shaped

Frank R. Stockton

something like a cuttlefish, with many arms which would cling to the bottom if any force were exerted to move the anchor. The other end of the chain was attached to the lower part of the buoy, and with powerful cranes the anchor was hoisted on deck, and when everything had been made ready the buoy, which had had the proper date cut upon it, was lowered into the water. Then the great anchor was dropped into the sea, as nearly as possible over the pole.

The sudden rush downward of the anchor and the chain caused the buoy to dip into the sea as if it were about to sink out of sight, but in a few moments it rose again, and the great sphere, half-way out of the water, floated proudly upon the surface of the polar sea.

Then came a great cheer, and Mrs. Block—who, having been assured that the whale had entirely disappeared, had come on deck—turned to her husband and remarked: "Now, Sammy, is there any earthly reason why we should not turn right around and go straight home? The pole's found, and the place is marked, and what more is there for us to do?"

But before her husband could answer her, Captain Hubbell lifted up his voice, which was full of spirit and enthusiasm.

"Messmates!" he cried, "we have touched at the pole, and we have anchored the buoy, and now let us go whalin'. It's thirty years since I saw one of them fish, and I never expected in all my born days I'd go a-whalin'."

The rest of the company on the Dipsey took no very great interest in the whaling cruise, but, on consultation with Mr. Clewe and Mrs. Raleigh at Sardis, it was decided that they ought by no means to leave the polar sea until they had explored it as thoroughly as circumstances would allow. Consequently the next day the Dipsey sailed away from the pole, leaving the buoy brightly floating on a gently rolling sea, its high-uplifted weather-vane glittering in the sun, with each of its ends always pointing bravely to the south.

CHAPTER XIV

A REGION OF NOTHINGNESS

In the office of the Works at Sardis, side by side at the table on which stood the telegraph instrument, Margaret Raleigh and Roland Clewe, receiving the daily reports from the Dipsey, had found themselves in such sympathy and harmony with the party they had sent out on this expedition that they too, in fancy, had slowly groped their way under the grim overhanging ice out into the open polar sea. They too had stood on the deck of the vessel which had risen like a spectre out of the waters, and in the cold, clear atmosphere had gazed about them at this hitherto unknown part of the world. They had thrilled with enthusiastic excitement when the ring on the deck of the Dipsey was placed over the actual location of the pole; they had been filled with anger when they heard of the conduct of Rovinski; and their souls had swelled with a noble love of country and pride in their own achievements when they heard that they, by their representative, had made the north pole a part of their native land. They had listened, scarcely breathing, to the stirring account of the anchoring of the great buoy to one end of the earth's axis, and they had exclaimed in amazement at the announcement that in the lonely waters of the pole whales were still to be found, when they were totally unknown in every other portion of the earth.

But now the stirring events in the arctic regions which had so held and enthralled them day by day had, after a time, ceased. Mr. Gibbs was engaged in making experiments, observations, and explorations, the result of which he would embody in carefully prepared reports, and Sammy's daily message promised to be rather monotonous. Roland Clewe felt the great importance of a thorough exploration and examination of the polar sea. The vessel he had sent out had reached this hitherto inaccessible region, but it was not at all certain that another voyage, even of the same kind, would be successful. Consequently he advised those in charge of the expedition not to attempt to return until the results of their work were as complete as possible. Should the arctic night overtake them before they left the polar sea, this would not interfere with their return in the same manner in which they had gone north, for in a submarine voyage artificial light would be necessary at any season. So, for a tune, Roland and Margaret withdrew in a great measure their thoughts from the vicinity of the pole, and devoted themselves to their work at home.

When Roland Clewe had penetrated with his Artesian ray as deeply into the earth beneath him as the photic power of his instrument would admit, he had applied all the available force of his establishment—the men working in relays day and night—to the manufacture of the instruments which should give increased power to the penetrating light, which he hoped would make visible to him the interior structure of the earth, up to this time as unknown to man as had been the regions of the poles.

Roland had devoted a great deal of time to the arrangement of a system of reflectors, by which he hoped to make it possible to look down into the cylinder of light produced by the Artesian ray without projecting any portion of the body of the observer into the ray. This had been done principally to provide against the possibility of a shock to Margaret,

Frank R. Stockton

such as he received when he beheld a man with the upper part of his body totally invisible, and a section of the other portion laid bare to the eye of a person standing in front of it. But his success had not been satisfactory. It was quite different to look directly down into that magical perforation at his feet, instead of studying the reflection of the same, indistinctly and uncertainly revealed by a system of mirrors.

Consequently the plan of reflectors was discarded, and Roland determined that the right thing to do was to take Margaret into his confidence and explain to her why he and she should not stand together and look down the course of the Artesian ray. She scolded him for not telling her all this before, and a permanent screen was erected around the spot on which the ray was intended to work, formed of Venetian blinds with fixed slats, so that the person inside could readily talk and consult with others outside without being seen by them.

As might well be supposed, this work with the "photic borer," as Clewe now called his instrument, was of absorbing interest. For a day or two after it was again put into operation Margaret and Roland could scarcely tear themselves away from it long enough for necessary sleep and meals, and several persons connected with the Works were frequently permitted to witness its wonderful operations.

Down, down descended that cylinder of light, until it had passed through all the known geological strata in that part of New Jersey, and had reached subterranean depths known to Clewe only by comparison and theory.

The apparent excavation had extended itself down so far that the disk at the bottom, although so brightly illuminated, was no longer clearly visible to the naked eye, and was rapidly decreasing in size on account of the perspective. But the telescopes which Clewe had provided easily overcame this difficulty. He was sure that it would be impossible for his light to penetrate to a depth which could not be made clearly visible by his telescopes.

It was a wonderful and weird sensation which came over those who stood, glass in hand, and gazed down the track of the Artesian ray. Far, far below them they saw that illuminated disk which revealed the character of the stratum which the light had reached. And yet they could not see the telescope which they held in their hands; they could not see their hands; they knew that their heads and shoulders were invisible. All observers except Clewe kept well back from the edge of the frightful hole of light down which they peered; and once, when the weight of the telescope which she held had caused Margaret to make an involuntary step forward, she gave a fearful scream, for she was sure she was going to fall into the bowels of the earth. Clewe, who stood always near by, with his hand upon the lever which controlled the ray, instantly shut off the light; and although Margaret was thus convinced that she stood upon commonplace ground, she came from within the screen, and did not for some time recover from the nervous shock occasioned by this accident of the imagination.

Clewe himself took great pleasure in making experiments connected with the relation of the observer to the action of the Artesian ray. For instance, he found that when standing and gazing down into the great photic perforation below him, he could see into it quite as well when he shut his eyes as when they were open; the light passing through his head made his eyelids invisible. He stood in the very centre of the circle of light and looked down through himself.

That this application of light which he had discovered would be of the greatest possible service in surgery, Roland Clewe well knew. By totally eliminating from view any portion of the human body so as to expose a section of said body which

Frank R. Stockton

it was desirable to examine, the interior structure of a patient could be studied as easily as the exterior, and a surgeon would be able to dissect a living being as easily as if the subject were a corpse. But Clewe did not now wish to make public the extraordinary adaptations of his discovery to the uses of the medical man and the surgeon. He was intent upon discovering, as far as was possible, the internal structure of the earth on which he dwelt, and he did not wish to interfere at present with this great and absorbing object by distracting his mind with any other application of his Artesian ray.

It is not intended to describe in detail the various stages of the progress of the Artesian ray into the subterranean regions. Sometimes it revealed strata colored red, yellow, or green by the presence of iron ore; sometimes it showed for a short distance a glittering disk, produced by the action of the light upon a deep-sunken reservoir of water; then it passed on, hour by hour, down, down into the eternal rocks.

When the Artesian ray had begun to work its way through the rocks, Margaret became less interested in observing its progress. Nothing new presented itself; it was one continual stony disk which she saw when she looked down into the shaft of light beneath her. Observation was becoming more and more difficult even to Roland Clewe, and at last he was obliged to set up a large telescope on a stand, and mount a ladder in order to use it.

Day after day the Artesian ray went downward, always revealing rock, rock, rock. The appliances for increased electric energy were working well, and Clewe was entirely satisfied with the operation of his photic borer.

One morning he came hurriedly to Margaret at her house, and announced with glistening eyes that his ray had now gone to a greater degree into the earth than man had ever yet reached.

"What have you found?" she asked, excitedly. "Rock, rock, rock," he answered. "This little State of ours rests upon a firm foundation."

Although Roland Clewe found his observations rather monotonous work, he was regular and constant at his post, and gave little opportunity to his steadily progressing cylinder of light to reach and pass unseen anything which might be of interest.

It was nearly a week after he had announced to Margaret that he had seen deeper into the earth than any man before him that he mounted his ladder to take his final observation for the night. When he looked through his telescope his eye was dazzled by a light which obliged him suddenly to close it and lift his head. At first he thought that he had reached the fabulous region of eternal fire, but this he knew to be absurd; and, besides, the light was not that of fire or heated substances. It was pale, colorless; and although dazzling at first, he found, when very cautiously he applied his eye again to the telescope, that it was not blinding. In fact, he could look at it as steadily as he could upon a clear sky.

But, gaze as he would, he could see nothing—nothing but light; subdued, soft, beautiful light. He knew the ray was passing steadily downward, for the mechanism was working with its accustomed regularity, but it revealed to him nothing at all. He could not understand it; his brain was dazed. He thought there might be something the matter with his eyesight. He got down from the ladder and hurriedly sent for Margaret, and when she came he begged her to look through the telescope and tell him what she saw. She went inside the screen, ascended the ladder, and looked down.

"It isn't anything," she called out presently. "It looks like lighter air; it can't be that. Perhaps there is something the matter with your telescope."

Clewe had thought of that, and as soon as she came out he examined the instrument, but the lenses were all right. There was nothing the matter with the telescope.

That night Roland Clewe spent in the lens-house, almost constantly at the telescope, but nothing did he see but a disk of soft, white light.

"The world can't be hollow!" he said to Margaret the next morning. "It can't be filled with air, or nothing, and my ray would not illuminate air or nothing. I cannot understand it. If you did not see what I see, I should think I was going crazy."

"Don't talk that way," exclaimed Margaret. "This may be some cavity which the ray will soon pass through, and then we shall come to the good old familiar rock again."

But Clewe could not be consoled in this way. He could see no reason why his ray acting upon the emptiness of a cavern should produce the effect he beheld. Moreover, if the ray had revealed a cavern of considerable extent he could not expect that it could now pass through it, for the limit of its operations was almost reached. His electric cumulators would cease to act in a few hours more. The ray had now descended more than fourteen miles—its limit was fifteen.

Margaret was greatly troubled because of the effect of this result of the light borer upon Roland. His disappointment was very great, and it showed itself in his face. His Artesian ray had gone down to a distance greater than had been sometimes estimated as the thickness of the earth's crust, and the result was of no value. Roland did not believe that the earth had a crust. He had no faith in the old-fashioned idea that the great central portion was a mass of molten matter, but he could not drive from his mind the conviction that his light had passed through the solid portion of the earth, and had emerged into something which was not solid, which was not liquid, which was in fact nothing.

All his labors had come to this: he had discovered that the various strata near the earth's surface rested upon a vast bed of rock, and that this bed of rock rested upon nothing. Of course it was not impossible that the arrangement of the substances which make up this globe was peculiar at this point, and that there was a great cavern fourteen miles below him; but why should such a cavern be filled with a light different from that which would be shown by his Artesian ray when shining upon any other substances, open air or solid matter?

He could go no deeper down—at least at present. If he could make an instrument of increased power, it would require many months to do it.

"But I will do it," said he to Margaret. "If this is a cavern, and if it has a bottom, I will reach it. I will go on and see what there is beyond. On such a discovery as I have made one can pass no conclusion whatever. If I cannot go farther, I need not have gone down at all."

"No," said Margaret, "I don't want you to go on—at least at present; you must wait. The earth will wait, and I want you to be in a condition to be able to wait also. You must now stop this work altogether. Stop doing anything; stop thinking about it. After a time—say early in winter—we can recommence operations with the Artesian ray; that is, if we think well to do so. You should stop this and take up something else. You have several enterprises which are very important and ought to be carried on. Take up one of them, and think no more for a few months of the nothingness which is fourteen miles below us."

It was not difficult for Roland Clewe to convince himself that this was very good advice. He resolved to shut up his lens-house entirely for a time, and think no more of the great work he had done within it, but apply himself to something which he had long neglected, and which would be a distraction and a recreation to his disappointed mind.

CHAPTER XV

THE AUTOMATIC SHELL

In a large building, not far from the lens-house in which Roland Clewe had pursued the experiments which had come to such a disappointing conclusion, there was a piece of mechanism which interested its inventor more than any other of his works, excepting of course the photic borer.

This was an enormous projectile, the peculiarity of which was that its motive power was contained within itself, very much as a rocket contains the explosives which send it upward. It differed, however, from the rocket or any other similar projectile, and many of its features were entirely original with Roland Clewe.

This extraordinary piece of mechanism, which was called the automatic shell, was of cylindrical form, eighteen feet in length and four feet in diameter. The forward end was conical and not solid, being formed of a number of flat steel rings, decreasing in size as they approached the point of the cone. When not in operation these rings did not touch one another, but they could be forced together by pressure on the point of the cone. This shell might contain explosives or not, as might be considered desirable, and it was not intended to fire it from a cannon, but to start it on its course from a long semi-cylindrical trough, which would be used simply to give

Frank R. Stockton

it the desired direction. After it had been started by a ram worked by an engine at the rear end of the trough, it immediately bean to propel itself by means of the mechanism contained within it.

But the great value of this shell lay in the fact that the moment it encountered a solid substance or obstruction of any kind its propelling power became increased. The rings which formed the cone on its forward end were pressed together, the electric motive power was increased in proportion to the pressure, and thus the greater the resistance to this projectile the greater became its velocity and power of progression, and its onward course continued until its self-containing force had been exhausted.

The power of explosives had reached, at this period, to so high a point that it was unnecessary to devise any increase in their enormous energy, and the only problems before the students of artillery practice related to methods of getting their projectiles to the points desired. Progress in this branch of the science had proceeded so far that an attack upon a fortified port by armored vessels was now considered as a thing of the past; and although there had been no naval wars of late years, it was believed that never again would there be a combat between vessels of iron or steel.

The recently invented magnetic shell made artillery practice against all vessels of iron a mere mechanical process, demanding no skill whatever. When one of these magnetic shells was thrown anywhere in the vicinity of an iron ship, the powerful magnetism developed within it instantly attracted it to the vessel, which was destroyed by the ensuing contact and explosion. Two ironclads meeting on the ocean need each to fire but one shell to be both destroyed. The inability of iron battle-ships to withstand this improvement in artillery had already set the naval architects of the world upon the work of constructing warships which would not attract the magnetic shell—which was effective even when laid on the bottoms of harbors—and Roland Clewe had been engaged in making plans and experiments for the construction of a paper man-of-war, which he believed would meet the requirements of the situation.

When Clewe determined to follow Margaret Raleigh's advice and give up for a time his work with the Artesian ray, his thoughts naturally turned to his automatic shell. Work upon this invention was now almost completed, but the great difficulty which its inventor expected to meet with was that of inducing his government to make a trial of it. Such a trial would be extremely expensive, involving probably the destruction of the shell, and he did not feel able or willing to experiment with it without governmental aid.

The shell was intended for use on land as well as at sea, against cities and great fortified structures, and Clewe believed that the automatic shell might be brought within fifty miles of a city, set up with its trough and ram, and projected in a level line towards its object, to which it would impel itself with irresistible power and velocity, through forests, hills, buildings, and everything, gaining strength from every opposition which stood in the direct line of its progress. Attacking fortifications from the sea, the vessel carrying this great projectile could operate at a distance beyond the reach of the magnetic shell.

Now that the automatic shell itself was finished, and nothing remained to be done but to complete the great steel trough in which it would lie, Roland Clewe found himself confronted with a business which was very hard and very distasteful to him. He must induce other people to do what he was not able to do himself. Unless his shell was put to a practical trial, it could be of no value to the world or to himself.

In one of the many conversations on the subject; Margaret

had suggested something which rapidly grew and developed in Roland's mind.

"It would be an admirable thing to tunnel mountains with," said she. "Of course I mean a large one, as thick through as a tunnel ought to be."

In less than a day Clewe had perfected an idea which he believed might be of practical service. For some time there had been talk of a new railroad in this part of the State, but one of the difficulties in the way was the necessity of making a tunnel or a deep cut through a small mountain. To go round this mountain would be objectionable for many reasons, and to go through it would be enormously expensive. Clewe knew the country well, and his soul glowed within him as he thought that here perhaps was an opportunity for him to demonstrate the value of his invention, not only as an agent in warfare, but as a wonderful assistant in the peaceful progress of the world.

There was no reason why such shells should not be constructed for the express purpose of making tunnels. Nothing could be better adapted for an experiment of this kind than the low mountain in question. If the shell passed through it at the desired point, there would be nothing beyond which could be injured, and it would then enter the end of a small chain of mountains, and might pass onward, as far as its motive power would carry it, without doing any damage whatever. Moreover, its course could be followed and it could be recovered.

Both Roland and Margaret were very enthusiastic in favor of this trial of the automatic shell, and they determined that if the railroad company would pay them a fair price if they should succeed in tunnelling the mountain, they would charge nothing should their experiment be a failure. Of course the tunnel the shell would make, if everything worked properly, would not be large enough for any practical use; but explosives might be placed along its length, which, if desired, would blow out that portion of the mountain which lay immediately above the tunnel, and this great cut could readily be enlarged to any desired dimensions.

Clewe would have gone immediately to confer with the secretary of the railroad company, with whom he was acquainted. but that gentleman was at the sea-side, and the business was necessarily postponed.

"Now," said Clewe to Margaret, "if I could do it, I'd like to take a run up to the polar sea and see for myself what they have discovered. Judging from Sammy's infrequent despatches, the party in general must be getting a little tired of Mr. Gibbs's experiments and soundings; but I should be intensely interested in them."

"I don't wonder," answered Margaret, "that they are getting tired; they have found the pole, and they want to come home. That is natural enough. But, for my part, I am very glad we can't run up there. Even if we had another Dipsey I should decidedly oppose it. I might agree that we should go to Cape Tariff, but I would not agree to anything more. You may discover poles if you want to, but you must do it by proxy."

At this moment an awful crash was heard. It came from the building containing the automatic shell. Clewe and Margaret started to their feet. They glanced at each other, and then both ran from the office at the top of their speed. Other people were running from various parts of the Works. There was no smoke; there was no dust. There had been no explosion, as Clewe had feared in his first alarm.

When they entered the building, Clewe and Margaret stood aghast. There were workmen shouting or standing with open mouths; others were running in. The massive scaffolding,

Frank R. Stockton

twenty feet in height, on which the shell had been raised so that the steel trough might be run under it, lay in splinters upon the ground. The great automatic shell itself had entirely disappeared.

For some moments no one said anything; all stood astounded, looking at the space where the shell had been. Then Clewe hurried forward. In the ground, amid the wreck of the scaffolding, was a circular hole about four feet in diameter. Clasping the hand of a man near him, he cautiously peered over the edge and looked down. It was dark and deep; he saw nothing.

Roland Clewe stepped back; he put his hands over his eyes and thought. Now he comprehended everything clearly. The weight of the shell had been too great for its supports. The forward part, which contained the propelling mechanism, was much heavier than the other end, and had gone down first, so that the shell had turned over and had fallen perpendicularly, striking the ground with the point of the cone. Then its tremendous propelling energy, infinitely more powerful than any dynamic force dreamed of in the preceding century, was instantly generated. The inconceivably rapid motion which forced it forward like a screw must have then commenced, and it had bored itself down deep into the solid earth.

"Roland, dear," said Margaret, stepping quietly up to him, tears on her pale countenance, "don't you think it can be hoisted up again?"

"I hope not," said he.

"Why do you say that?" she asked, astonished.

"Because," he answered, "if it has not penetrated far enough into the earth to make it utterly out of our power to get it again, the thing is a failure."

"More than that," thought Margaret; "if it has gone down entirely out of our reach, the thing is a failure all the same, for I don't believe he can ever be induced to make another."

CHAPTER XVI

THE TRACK OF THE SHELL

During the course of his inventive life Roland Clewe had become accustomed to disappointments; he was very much afraid, indeed, that he was beginning to expect them. If that really happened, there would be an end to his career.

But when he spoke in this way to Margaret, she almost scolded him.

"How utterly absurd it is," she said, "for a man who has just discovered the north pole to sit down in an arm-chair and talk in that way!"

"I didn't discover it," he said; "it was Sammy and Gibbs who found the pole. As for me—I don't suppose I shall ever see it."

"I am not so sure of that," she said. "We may yet invent a telescope which shall curve its reflected rays over the rotundity of the earth and above the highest icebergs, so that you and I may sit here and look at the waters of the pole gently splashing around the great buoy."

"And charge a dollar apiece to all other people who would like to look at the pole, and so we might make much money," said he. "But I must really go and do something; I shall go crazy if I sit here idle."

Margaret knew that the loss of the shell was the greatest blow that Roland had ever yet received. His ambitions as a scientific inventor were varied, but she was well aware that for some years he had considered it of great importance to do something which would bring him in money enough to go on with his investigations and labors without depending entirely upon her for the necessary capital. If he could have tunnelled a mountain with this shell, or if he had but partially succeeded in so doing, money would have come to him. He would have made his first pecuniary success of any importance.

"What are you going to do, Roland?" said she, as he rose to leave the room.

"I am going to find the depth of the hole that shell has made. It ought to be filled up, and I must calculate how many loads of earth and stones it will take to do it."

That afternoon he came to Mrs. Raleigh's house.

"Margaret," he exclaimed, "I have lowered a lead into that hole with all the line attached which we have got on the place, and we can touch no bottom. I have telegraphed for a lot of sounding-wire, and I must wait until it shall arrive before I do anything more."

"You must be very, very careful, Roland, when you are doing that work," said Margaret. "Suppose you should fall in!"

"I have provided against that," said he. "I have laid a floor over the hole with only a small opening in it, so there is no danger. And another curious thing I must tell you-our line is not wet: we have struck no water!"

When Margaret visited the Works the next day she found Roland Clewe and a number of workmen surrounding the flooring which had been laid over the hole. They were sounding with a windlass which carried an immense reel of wire. The wire was extremely thin, but the weight of that portion of it which had already been unwound was so great that four men were at the handles of the windlass.

Roland came to meet Margaret as she entered.

"The lead has gone down six miles," he said, in a low voice, "and we have not touched the bottom yet."

"Impossible!" she cried. "Roland, it cannot be! The wire must be coiling itself up somewhere. It is incredible! The lead cannot have gone down so far!"

"Leads have gone down as far as that before this," said he. "Soundings of more than six miles have been obtained at sea."

She went with him and stood near the windlass. For an hour she remained by his side, and still the reel turned steadily and the wire descended into the hole.

"Shall you surely know when it gets to the bottom?" said she.

"Yes," he answered. "When the electric button under the lead shall touch anything solid, or even anything fluid, this bell up here will ring."

She stayed until she could stay no longer. She knew it would be of no use to urge Roland to leave the windlass. Very early the next morning a note was brought to her before she was up, and on it was written:

"We have touched bottom at a depth of fourteen and an eighth miles."

When Roland came to Mrs. Raleigh's house, about nine o'clock that morning, his face was pale and his whole form trembled.

"Margaret," he cried, "what are we going to do about it? It is wonderful; I cannot appreciate it. I have had all the men up in the office this morning and pledged them to secrecy. Of course they won't keep their promises, but it was all that I could do. I can think of no particular damage which would come to me if this thing were known, but I cannot bear that the public should get hold of it until I know something myself. Margaret, I don't know anything."

"Have you had your breakfast?" she asked.

"No," he said; "I haven't thought of it."

"Did you eat anything last night?"

"I don't remember," he answered.

"Now I want you to come into the dining-room," said she. "I had a light breakfast some time ago, and I am going to eat another with you. I want you to tell me something. There was a man here the other day with a patent machine for making button-holes—you know the old-fashioned button-holes are coming in again—and if this is a good invention it ought to sell, for nearly everybody has forgotten how to make button-holes in the old way."

"Oh, nonsense!" said Roland. "How can you talk of such things? I can't take my mind—"

"I know you can't," she interrupted. "You are all the time

Frank R. Stockton

thinking of that everlasting old hole in the ground. Well, I am tired of it; do let us talk of something else."

Margaret Raleigh was much more than tired of that phenomenal hole in the earth which had been made by the automatic shell; she was frightened by it. It was something terrible to her; she had scarcely slept that night, and she needed breakfast and change of thought as much as Roland.

But it was not long before she found that it was impossible to turn his thoughts from that all-absorbing subject. All she could do was to endeavor to guide them into quiet channels.

"What are you going to do this morning?" she asked, towards the close of the breakfast.

"I am going to try to take the temperature of that shaft at various points," said he.

"That will be an excellent thing," she answered; "you may make valuable discoveries; but I should think the heat at that great depth would be enough to melt your thermometers."

"It did not melt my lead or my sounding-wire," said he. And as he said these words her heart fell.

The temperature of this great perforation was taken at many points, and when Roland brought to Margaret the statement of the height of the mercury at the very bottom she was astounded and shocked to find that it was only eighty-three degrees.

"This is terrible!" she ejaculated.

"What do you mean?" he asked in surprise. "That is not hot. Why, it is only summer weather."

But she did not think it terrible because it was so hot; the fact that it was so cool had shocked her. In such temperature one could live! A great source of trust and hope had been taken from her.

"Roland," she said, sinking into a chair, "I don't understand this at all. I always thought that it became hotter and hotter as one went down into the earth; and I once read that at twenty miles below the surface, if the heat increased in proportion as it increased in a mine, the temperature must be over a thousand degrees Fahrenheit. Your instrument could not have registered properly; perhaps it never went all the way down; and perhaps it is all a mistake. It may be that the lead did not go down so far as you think."

He smiled; he was becoming calmer now, for he was doing something: he was obtaining results.

"Those ideas about increasing heat at increasing depths are old-fashioned, Margaret," he said. "Recent science has given us better theories. It is known that there is great heat in the interior of the earth, and it is also known that the transmission of this heat towards the surface depends upon the conductivity of the rocks in particular locations. In some places the heat comes very near the surface, and in others it is very, very far down. More than that, the temperature may rise as we go down into the earth and afterwards fall again. There may be a stratum of close-grained rock, possibly containing metal, coming up from the interior in an oblique direction and bringing the heat towards the surface; then below that there may be vast regions of other rocks which do not readily conduct heat, and which do not originate in heated portions of the earth's interior. When we reach these, we must find the temperature lower, as a matter of course. Now I have really done this. A little over five miles down my thermometer registered ninety-one, and after that it began to fall a little. But the rocks under us are poor conductors of

Frank R. Stockton

heat; and, moreover, it is highly probable that they have no near communication with the source of internal heat."

"I thought these things were more exact and regular," said she; "I supposed if you went down a mile in one place, you would find it as hot as you would in another."

"Oh no," said he. "There is nothing regular or exact in nature; even our earth is not a perfect sphere. Nature is never mathematically correct. You must always allow for variations. In some parts of the earth its heated core, or whatever it is, must be very, very far down."

At this moment a happy thought struck Margaret.

"How easy it would be, Roland, for you to examine this great hole! I can do it; anybody can do it. It's perfectly amazing when you think of it. All you have to do is to take your Artesian, ray machine into that building and set it over the hole; then you can light the whole interior, all the way down to the bottom, and with a telescope you can see everything that is in it."

"Yes," said he; "but I think I can do it better than that. It would be very difficult to transfer the photic borer to the other building, and I can light up the interior perfectly well by means of electric lights. I can even lower a camera down to the very bottom and take photographs of the interior."

"Why, that would be perfectly glorious!" cried Margaret, springing to her feet, an immense relief coming to her mind with the thought that to examine this actual shaft it would not be necessary for anybody to go down into it.

"I should go to work at that immediately," said he, "but I must have a different sort of windlass—one that shall be moved by an engine. I will rig up the big telescope too, so that we can look down when we have lighted up the bottom."

It required days to do all that Roland Clewe had planned. A great deal of the necessary work was done in his own establishment, and much machinery besides was sent from New York. When all was ready many experiments were made with the electric lights and camera, and photographs of inexpressible value and interest were taken at various points on the sides of this wonderful perpendicular tunnel.

At last Clewe was prepared to photograph the lower portion of the shaft. With a peculiar camera and a powerful light five photographs were taken of the very bottom of the great shaft, four in horizontal directions and one immediately below the camera. When these photographs were printed by the improved methods then in vogue, Clewe seized the pictures and examined them with eager haste. For some moments he stood silent, his eyes fixed upon the photographs as if there was nothing else in this world; but all he saw on each was an irregular patch of light. He thrust the prints aside, and in a loud, sharp voice he gave orders to bring the great telescope and set it up above the hole. The light was still at the bottom, and the instant the telescope was in position Clewe mounted the stepladder and directed the instrument downward. In a few moments he gave an exclamation, and then he came down from the ladder so rapidly that he barely missed falling. He went into his office and sent for Margaret. When she came he showed her the photographs.

"See!" he said. "What I have found is nothing; even a camera shows nothing, and when I look down through the glass I see nothing. It is just what the Artesian ray showed me; it is nothing at all!"

"I should think," said she, speaking very slowly, "that if your sounding-lead had gone down into nothing, it would have continued to go down indefinitely. What was there to stop it if there is nothing there?"

"Margaret," said he, "I don't know anything about it. That is the crushing truth. I can find out nothing at all. When I look down through the earth by means of the Artesian ray I reach a certain depth and then I see a void; when I look down through a perfectly open passage to the same depth, I still see a void."

"But, Roland," said Margaret, holding in her hand the view taken of the bottom of the shaft, "what is this in the middle of the proof? It is darker than the rest, but it seems to be all covered up with mistiness. Have you a magnifying-glass?"

Roland found a glass, and seized the photograph. He had forgotten his usual courtesy.

"Margaret," he cried, "that dark thing is my automatic shell! It is lying on its side. I can see the greater part of it. It is not in the hole it made itself; it is in a cavity. It has turned over, and lies horizontally; it has bored down into a cave, Margaret —into a cave—a cave with a solid bottom—a cave made of light!"

"Nonsense!" said Margaret. "Caves cannot be made of light; the light that you see comes from your electric lamp."

"Not at all!" he cried. "If there was anything there, the light of my lamp would show it. During the whole depth of the shaft the light showed everything and the camera showed everything; you can see the very texture of the rocks; but when the camera goes to the bottom, when it enters this space into which the shaft plainly leads, it shows nothing at all, except what I may be said to have put there. I see only my great shell surrounded by light, resting on light!"

"Roland," said Margaret, "you are crazy! Perhaps it is water which fills that cave, or whatever it is."

"Not at all," said Roland. "It presents no appearance of water, and when the camera came up it was not wet. No; it is a cave of light."

He sat for some minutes silently gazing out of the window. Margaret drew her chair closer to him. She took one of his hands in both of hers.

"Look at me, Roland!" she said. "What are you thinking about?"

He turned his face upon her, but said nothing. She looked straight into his eyes, and she needed no Artesian ray to enable her to see through them into his innermost brain. She saw what was filling that brain; it was one great, over-powering desire to go down to the bottom of that hole, to find out what it was that he had discovered.

"Margaret, you hurt me!" he exclaimed, suddenly. In the intensity of the emotion excited by what she had discovered, her finger-nails had nearly penetrated through his skin. She had felt as if she would hold him and hold him forever, but she released his hand.

"We haven't talked about that button-hole machine," she said. "I want your opinion of it." To her surprise, Roland began immediately to discuss the new invention of which she had spoken, and asked her to describe it. He was not at all anxious now to tell Margaret what he was thinking of in connection with the track of the shell.

Frank R. Stockton

CHAPTER XVII

CAPTAIN HUBBELL DECLINES TO GO WHALING

The most impatient person on board the Dipsey was Captain Jim Hubbell. Sarah Block was also very anxious to go home as soon as matters could be arranged for the return journey, and she talked a great deal of the terrible fate which would be sure to overtake them if they should be so unfortunate as to stay until the season of the arctic night; but, after all, she was not as impatient as Captain Hubbell. She simply wanted to go home; but he not only greatly desired to return to his wife and family, but he wanted to do something else before he started south; he wanted to go whaling. He considered himself the only man in the whole world who had a chance to go whaling, and he chafed as he thought of the hindrances which Mr. Gibbs was continually placing in the way of this, the grandest of all sports.

Mr. Gibbs was a mild man, and rather a quiet one; but he thoroughly understood the importance of the investigations he was pursuing in the polar sea, and placed full value upon the opportunity which had come to him of examining the wonders of a region hitherto locked up from civilized man. Captain Hubbell was astonished to find that Mr. Gibbs was as hard and unyielding as an iceberg during his explorations and soundings. It was of no use to talk to him of whaling; he had work before him, and he must do it.

But the time came when Mr. Gibbs relented. The Dipsey had sailed around the whole boundary of the polar sea; observations, surveys, and maps had been made, and the general geography of the region had been fairly well determined. There still remained some weeks of the arctic day, and it was desirable that they should begin their return journey during that time; so Mr. Gibbs informed Captain Jim that if he wanted to do a little whaling, he would like him to lose no time.

Almost from the time of their arrival in the polar sea the subject of whales had greatly interested everybody on the Dipsey. Even Rovinski, who had been released from his confinement after a few days, because he had really committed no actual crime except that of indulging in overleaping ambition, had spent every available minute of leisure in looking for whales. It was strange that nothing in this Northern region interested the people on the Dipsey (with the sole exception of Mr. Gibbs) so much as these great fish, which seemed to be the only visible inhabitants of the polar solitudes. There were probably white bears somewhere on the icy shores about them, but they never showed themselves; and if birds were there, they did not fly over that sea.

There was reason to suppose that there were a good many whales in the polar sea. Wherever our party sailed, lay to, or anchored for a time, they were very sure, before long, to see a whale curving his shining black back into the light, or sending two beautiful jets of water up into the air. Whenever a whale was seen, somebody on board was sure to remark that these creatures in this part of the world seemed to be very tame. It was not at all uncommon to see one disport himself at no great distance from the vessel for an hour or more.

"If I could get among a school of whales anywhere around

Nantucket and find 'em as tame as these fellers," said Captain Jim, "I'd give a boom to the whale-oil business that it hasn't had for forty years."

But not long before Mr. Gibbs told the captain that he might go whaling if he felt like it, the old sailor had experienced a change of mind. He had become a most ardent student of whales. In his very circumscribed experience when a young man he had seen whales, but they had generally been a long way off; and as the old-fashioned method of rowing after them in boats had even then been abandoned in favor of killing them by means of the rifled cannon, Captain Hubbell had not seen very much of these creatures until they had been towed alongside. But now he could study whales at his leisure. It was seldom that he had to wait very long before he would see one near enough for him to examine it with a glass, and he never failed to avail himself of such opportunities.

The consequence of this constant and careful inspection was the conclusion in Captain Hubbell's mind that there was only one whale in the polar sea. He had noticed, and others had noticed, that they never saw two at once, and the captain had used his glass so often and so well that one morning he stamped his foot upon the deck and said to Sammy:

"I believe that's the same whale over and over and over ag'in. I know him like a book; he has his ways and his manners, and it isn't reasonable to suppose that every whale has the same ways and manners. He comes just so near the vessel, and then he stops and blows. Then he suns his back for a while, and then he throws up his flukes and sounds. He does that as regular as if he was a polar clock. I know the very shape of his flukes; and two or three days ago, as he was soundin', I thought that the tip of the upper one looked as if it had been damaged—as if he had broken it floppin' about in some tight place; and ever since, when I have seen a whale, I have looked for the tip of that upper fluke, and there's that same old break. Every time I have looked I have found it. It can't be that there are a lot o' whales in here and each one of 'em with a battered fluke."

"That does look sort o' queer," said Sammy, reflectively.

"Sammy Block," said Captain Jim, impressively, "it's my opinion that there's only one whale in this here polar sea; an', more than that, it's my opinion that there's only one whale in this world, an' that that feller we've seen is the one! Samuel Block, he's the last whale in the whole world! Now you know that I wanted to go a-whalin'—that's natural enough—but since Mr. Gibbs has got through, and has said that I could take this vessel an' go a-whalin' if I wanted to—which would be easy enough, for we have got guns aboard which would kill any right-whale—I don't want to go. I don't want to lay on my dyin' bed an' think that I'm the man that killed the last whale in the world. I'm commandin' this vessel, and I sail it wherever Mr. Gibbs tells me to sail it; but if he wants the bones of a whale to take home as a curiosity, an' tells me to sail this vessel after that whale, I won't do it."

"I'm with you there," said Sammy. "I have been thinkin' while you was talkin', an' it's my opinion that it's not only the last whale in the world, but it's purty nigh tame. I believe it's so glad to see some other movin' creature in this lonely sea that it wants to keep company with us all the time. No, sir, I wouldn't have anything to do with killin' that fish!"

The opinions of the captain and Sammy were now communicated to the rest of the company on board, and nearly all of them thought that they had had such an idea themselves. The whale certainly looked very familiar every time he showed himself.

To Mr. Gibbs this lonely creature, if he were such, now

became an object of intense interest. It was evidently a specimen of the right-whale, once common in the Northern seas, skeletons of which could be seen in many museums. Nothing would be gained to science by his capture, and Mr. Gibbs agreed with the others that it would be a pity to harm this, the last of his race.

In thinking and talking over the matter Mr. Gibbs formed a theory which he thought would explain the presence of this solitary whale in the polar sea. He thought it very likely that it had gotten under the ice and had pursued its northern journey very much as the Dipsey had pursued hers, and had at last emerged, as she had, into the polar sea at a place perhaps as shallow as that where the submarine vessel came out from under the ice.

"And if that's the case," said Captain Hubbell, "it is ten to one that he has not been able to get out again, and has found himself here caught just as if he was in a trap. Fishes don't like to swim into tight places. They may do it once, but they don't want to do it again. It is this disposition that makes 'em easy to catch in traps. I believe you are right, Mr. Gibbs. I believe this whale has got in here and can't get out—or, at least, he thinks he can't—and nobody knows how long it's been since he first got in. It may have been a hundred years ago. There's plenty o' little fish in these waters for him to eat, and he's the only one there is to feed."

The thought that in this polar sea with themselves was a great whale, which was probably here simply because he could not get out, had a depressing effect upon the minds of the party on the Dipsey. There was perhaps no real reason why they should fear the fate of the great fish, but, after all, this subject was one which should be very seriously considered. The latter part of their passage under the ice had been very hazardous. Had they struck a sharp rock below them, or had they been pierced by a jagged mass of ice above them, there probably would have been a speedy end of the expedition; and now, having come safely out of that dangerous shallow water, they shrank from going into it again.

It was the general opinion that if they would sail a considerable distance to the eastward they could not fail to find a deep channel by which the waters of this sea communicated with Baffin's Bay; but in this case they would be obliged to leave the line of longitude by which they had safely travelled from Cape Tariff to the pole and seek another route southward, along some other line, which would end their journey they knew not where.

"I am cold," said Sarah Block. "At first I got along all right, with all these furs, and goin' down-stairs every time I felt chilly, but the freezin' air is beginnin' to go into my very bones like needles; and if winter is comin' on, and it's goin' to be worse than this, New Jersey is the place for me. But there's one thing that chills my blood clammier than even the cold weather, and that is the thought of that whale follerin' us. If we get down into those shaller places under the ice an' he takes it into his head to come along, he'll be worse than a bull in a china-shop. I don't mean to say that I think he'll want to do us any harm, for he has never shown any sign of such a feelin', but if he takes to bouncin' and thrashin' when he scratches himself on any rocks, it'll be a bad box for us to be in."

None of the others shared these special fears of Mrs. Block, but they were all as much disinclined as she was to begin another submarine voyage in the shallow waters which they had been so glad to leave.

It was believed, from the general contour of the surrounding region, that if the ice were all melted away it would be seen that a cape projected from the American continent eastward at the point where they had entered the polar sea, and that it was in crossing the submerged continuation of this cape that they had found the shallow water. Beyond and southward they knew that the water was deep and safe. If they could reach that portion of the sea without crossing the shallow point, they would have no fears regarding their return voyage. They knew how far south it was that that deep water lay, and the questions before them related to the best means of reaching it.

At a general council of officers, Sammy and Captain Hubbell both declared that they were not willing to take any other path homeward except one which led along the seventieth line of longitude. That had brought them safely up, and it would take them safely down. If they went under the ice at some point eastward, how were they to find the seventieth line of longitude? They could not take observations down there; and they might have to go south on some other line, which would take them nobody knew where. Mr. Gibbs said little, but he believed that it would be well to go back the way they came.

At last a plan was proposed by Mr. Marcy, and adopted without dissent. The whole country which lay in the direction they wished to travel seemed to be an immense plain of ice and snow, with mountains looming up towards the west and in the far southeast. In places great slabs of ice seemed to be piled up into craggy masses, but in general the surface of the country was quite level, indicating underlying water. In fact, a little east of the point where they had entered the polar sea great cracks and reefs, some of them extending nearly a mile inward, broke up the shore line. The party on the Dipsey were fully able to travel over smooth ice and frozen snow, for this contingency had been thought of and provided for; but to take the Dipsey on an overland journey would, of course, be impossible. By Mr. Marcy's plan, however, it was thought that it would be quite feasible for the Dipsey to sail inland until she had reached a point where they were sure the deep sea lay serenely beneath the ice around them.

Frank R. Stockton

CHAPTER XVIII

Mr. MARCY'S CANAL

The twelve men and the one woman on board the Dipsey, now lying at anchor in the polar sea, were filled with a warming and cheering ardor as they began their preparations for the homeward journey, although these preparations included what was to all of them a very painful piece of work. It was found that it would be absolutely necessary to disengage themselves from the electric cord which in all their voyaging in these desolate arctic regions, under water and above water, had connected them with the Works of Roland Clewe at Sardis, New Jersey. A sufficient length of this cord, almost too slight to be called cable, to reach from Cape Tariff to the pole, with a margin adequate for all probable emergencies, had been placed on board the Dipsey, and it was expected that on her return these slender but immensely strong wires would be wound up, instead of being let out, and so still connect the vessel with Mr. Clewe's office.

But the Dipsey had sailed in such devious ways and in so many directions that she had laid a great deal of the cable upon the bottom of the polar sea, and it would be difficult, or perhaps impossible, to sail back over her previous tracks and take it up again; and there was not enough of it left for her to proceed southward very far and still keep up her telegraphic communication. Consequently it was considered best, upon starting southward, that they should cut loose from all connection with their friends and the rest of the world. They would have to do this anyway in a short time. If they left the end of the wire in some suitable position on the coast of the polar sea, it might prove of subsequent advantage to science, whereas if they cut loose when they were submerged in the ocean, this cable from Cape Tariff to the pole must always be absolutely valueless. It was therefore determined to build a little house, for which they had the material, and place therein a telegraph instrument connected with the wire, and provided with one of the Collison batteries, which would remain in working order with a charge sufficient to last for forty years, and this, with a ground-wire run down through the ice to the solid earth, might make telegraphic communication possible to some subsequent visitor to the pole.

But apart from the necessity of giving up connection with Sardis, the journey did not seem like such a strange and solemn progress through unknown regions as the northern voyage had been. If they could get themselves well down into the deep sea at a point on the seventieth line of longitude, they would sail directly south with every confidence of emerging safely into Baffin's Bay.

The latest telegrams between Sardis and the polar sea were composed mostly of messages of the warmest friendship and encouragement. If Mr. Clewe and Mrs. Raleigh felt any fears as to the success of the first part of the return journey, they showed no signs of them, and Sammy never made any reference to his wife's frequently expressed opinion that there was good reason to believe that the end of this thing would be that the Dipsey, with everybody on board of her, would suddenly, by one of those mishaps which nobody can prevent, be blown into fine dust.

Mr. Marcy's plan was a very simple one. The Dipsey carried

Frank R. Stockton

a great store of explosive appliances of various patterns and of the most improved kinds, and some of them of immense power, and Mr. Marcy proposed that a long line of these should be laid over the level ice and then exploded. The ice below them would be shivered into atoms, and he believed that an open channel might thus be made, through which the Dipsey might easily proceed. Then another line of explosives would be laid ahead of the vessel, and the length of the canal increased. This would be a slow method of proceeding, but it was considered a sure one.

As to the progress over the snow and ice of those who were to lay the lines of shells, that would be easy enough. It had been supposed that it might be necessary for the party to make overland trips, and for this purpose twenty or more electric-motor sledges had been provided. These sledges were far superior to any drawn by dogs or reindeer; each one of them, mounted on broad runners of aluminium, was provided with a small engine, charged at the vessel with electricity enough to last a week, and was propelled by means of a light metal wheel with sharp points upon its outer rim. This wheel was under the fore part of the sledge, and, revolving rapidly, its points caught in the ice or frozen snow and propelled the sledge at a good rate of speed. The wheel could be raised or lowered, so that its points should take more or less hold of the ice, according as circumstances demanded. In descending a declivity it could be raised entirely, so that the person on the sledge might coast, and it could at any time be brought down hard to act as a brake.

As soon as it was possible to get everything in order, a party of six men, on electric sledges, headed by Mr. Marcy, started southward over the level ice, carrying with them a number of shells, which were placed in a long line, and connected by an electric wire with the Dipsey. When the party had returned and the shells were exploded, the most sanguine anticipations of Mr. Marcy were realized. A magnificent canal three miles long lay open to the south.

Now the anchor of the Dipsey was weighed, and our party bade farewell to the polar sea. The great ball buoy, with its tall pole and weathervane, floated proudly over the northern end of the earth's axis. The little telegraph-house was all in order, and made as secure as possible, and under it the Dipsey people made a "cache" of provisions, leaving a note in several languages to show what they had done.

"If the whale wants to come ashore to get somethin' to eat and send a message, why, here's his chance!" said Sammy; "but it strikes me that if any human beings ever reach this pole again, they won't come the way we came, and they'll not see this little house, for it won't take many snow-storms— even if they are no worse than some of those we have seen— to cover it up out o' sight."

"I don't believe the slightest good will ever result on account of leaving this instrument here," said Mr. Gibbs; "but it seemed the right thing to do, and I would not be satisfied to go away and leave the useless end of the cable in these regions. We will set up the highest rod we have by the little house, and then we can do no more."

When the Dipsey started, everybody on board looked over the stern to see if they could catch a glimpse of their old companion, the whale. Nearly all of them were sorry that it was necessary to go away and desert this living being in his lonely solitude. They had not entered the canal when they saw the whale. Two tall farewell spouts rose into the air, and then his tail with its damaged fluke was lifted aloft and waved in a sort of gigantic adieu. Cheers and shouts of good-bye came from the Dipsey, and the whale disappeared from their sight.

"I hope he won't come up under us," said Mrs. Block. "But I

don't believe he will do that. He always kept at a respectful distance, and as long as we are goin' to sail in a canal, I wouldn't mind in the least if he followed us. But as for goin' under water with him—I don't want anybody to speak of it."

Our exploring party now found their arctic life much more interesting than it had lately been, for, from time to time, they were all enabled to leave the vessel and travel, if not upon solid land, upon very solid ice. The Dipsey carried several small boats, and even Sarah Block frequently landed and took a trip upon a motor sledge. Sometimes the ice was rough, or the frozen snow was piled up into hillocks, and in such cases it was easy enough to walk and draw the light sledges; but as a general thing the people on the sledges were able to travel rapidly and pleasantly. The scenery was rather monotonous, with its everlasting stretches of ice and snow, but in the far distance the mountains loomed up in the beautiful colors given them by an arctic atmosphere, and the rays of the sun still brightened the landscape at all hours. Occasionally animals, supposed to be arctic foxes, were seen at a great distance, and there were those in the company who declared that they had caught sight of a bear. But hunting was not encouraged. The party had no need of fresh meat, and there was important work to be done which should not be interfered with by sporting expeditions.

There were days of slow progress, but of varied and often exciting experiences, for sometimes the line of Mr. Marcy's canal lay through high masses of ice, and here the necessary blasting was often of a very startling character. They expected to cease their overland journey before they reached the mountains, which on the south and west were piled up much nearer to them than those in other quarters, but they were surprised to find their way stopped much sooner than they had expected it would be by masses of icebergs, which stood up in front of them out of the snowy plain.

When they were within a few miles of these glittering eminences they ceased further operations and held a council. It was perfectly possible to blow a great hole in the ice and descend into the sea at this point, but they would have preferred going farther south before beginning their submarine voyage. To the eastward of the icebergs they could see with their glasses great patches of open water, and this would have prevented the making of a canal around the icebergs, for it would have been impossible to survey the route on sledges or to lay the line of bombs.

A good deal of discussion followed, during which Captain Hubbell strongly urged the plan of breaking a path to the open water, and finding out what could be done in the way of sailing south in regular nautical fashion. If the Dipsey could continue her voyage above water he was in favor of her doing it, but even Captain Jim Hubbell could give no good reason for believing that if the vessel got into the open water the party would not be obliged to go into winter-quarters in these icy regions; for in a very few weeks the arctic winter would be upon them. Once under the water, they would not care whether it was light or dark, but in the upper air it would be quite another thing.

So Captain Hubbell's plan was given up, but it was generally agreed that it would be a very wise thing, before they took any further steps, to ascend one of the icebergs in front of them and see what was on the other side.

The mountain-climbing party consisted of Mr. Gibbs, Mr. Marcy, and three of the most active of the men. Sammy Block wanted to go with them, but his wife would not allow him to do it.

"You can take possession of poles, Sammy," said she, "for that is the thing you are good at, but when it comes to slidin' down icebergs on the small of your back you are out of

Frank R. Stockton

place; and if I get that house that Mr. Clewe lives in now, but which he is goin' to give up when he gets married, I don't want to live there alone. I can't think of nothin' dolefuler than a widow with a polar rheumatism, and that's what I'm pretty sure I'm goin' to have."

The ascent of the nearest iceberg was not such a difficult piece of work as it would have been in the days when Sammy Block and Captain Hubbell were boys. The climbers wore ice-shoes with leather suckers on the soles, such as the feet of flies are furnished with, so that it was almost impossible for them to slip; and when they came to a sloping surface, where it was too steep for them to climb, they made use of a motor sledge furnished with a wheel different from the others. Instead of points, this wheel had on its outer rim a series of suckers, similar to those upon the soles of the shoes of the party. As the wheel, which was of extraordinary strength, revolved, it held its rim tightly to whatever surface it was pressed against, without reference to the angle of said surface. In 1941, with such a sledge, Martin Gallinet, a Swiss guide, ascended seventy-five feet of a perpendicular rock face on Monte Rosa. The sledge, slowly propelled by its wheel, went up the face of the rock as if it had been a fly climbing up a pane of glass, and Gallinet, suspended below this sledge by a strap under his arms, was hauled to the top of the precipice.

It was not necessary to climb any such precipices in ascending an iceberg, but there were some steep slopes, and up these the party were safely carried, one by one, by what they called their Fly-foot Sledge.

After an hour or two of climbing, our party safely reached the topmost point of the iceberg, and began to gaze about them. They soon found that beyond them there were other peaks and pinnacles, and that it would have been difficult to make a circuit which would enable them to continue Mr.

Marcy's plan of a canal along the level ice. Far beyond them, to the south, ice hills and ice mountains were scattered here and there.

Suddenly Mr. Gibbs gave a shout of surprise.

"I have been here before," said he.

"Of course you have," replied Mr. Marcy. "This is Lake Shiver. Don't you see, away over there on the other side of the open water below us, that little dark spot in the icy wall? That is the frozen polar bear. Take your glass and see if it isn't."

CHAPTER XIX

THE ICY GATEWAY

When Mr. Gibbs and his party returned to the Dipsey, after descending the iceberg, their report created a lively sensation.

"Why, it's like goin' home," said Mrs. Block. "Perhaps I may find my shoes."

It was not a very strange thing that they should have again met with this little ice-locked lake, for they had endeavored to return by a route as directly south as the other had been directly north. But no one had expected to see the lake again, and they were not only surprised, but pleased and encouraged. Here was a spot where they knew the water was deep enough for perfectly safe submarine navigation, and if they could start here under the ice they would feel quite sure that they would meet with no obstacles on the rest of their voyage.

As there was no possible entrance to this lake from the point where the Dipsey now lay at the end of her canal, Sammy proposed that they should make a descent into the water at the place where they were, if, after making soundings, they should find the depth sufficient. Then they might proceed southward as well as if they should start from Lake Shiver.

But this did not suit Mr. Gibbs. He had a very strong desire to reach the waters of the little lake, because he knew that at their bottom lay the telegraphic cable which he had been obliged to abandon, and he had thought he might be able to raise this cable and re-establish telegraphic communication with Cape Tariff and New Jersey.

Sammy thought that Mr. Gibbs's desire could be accomplished by sinking into the water in which they now lay and sailing under the icebergs to the lake, but Mr. Gibbs did not favor this. He was afraid to go under the icebergs. To be sure, they had already sailed under one of them when the Dipsey had made her way northward from the lake, but they had found that the depth of water varied very much in different places, and the icebergs in front of them might be heavier, and therefore more deeply sunken, than those which they had previously passed under.

If it were possible to extend their canal to Lake Shiver, Mr. Gibbs wanted to do it, but if they should fail in this, then, of course, they would be obliged to go down at this or some adjacent spot.

"It's all very well," said Captain Hubbell, who was a little depressed in spirits because the time was rapidly approaching when he would no longer command the vessel, "but it's one thing to blow a canal through fields of flat ice, and another to make it all the way through an iceberg; but if you think you can do it, I am content. I'd like to sail above water just as far as we can go."

Mr. Gibbs had been studying the situation, and some ideas relating to the solution of the problem before him were forming themselves in his mind. At last he hit upon a plan which he thought might open the waters of Lake Shiver to the Dipsey, and, as it would not take very long to test the value of his scheme, it was determined to make the experiment.

Frank R. Stockton

There were but few on board who did not know that if a needle were inserted into the upper part of a large block of ice, and were then driven smartly into it, the ice would split. Upon this fact Mr. Gibbs based his theory of making an entrance to the lake.

A climbing party, larger than the previous one, set out for the iceberg, carrying with them, on several sledges, a long and heavy iron rod, which was a piece of the extra machinery on the Dipsey, and some explosives of a special kind.

When the iceberg had been reached, several of the party ascended with a hoisting apparatus, and with this the rod was hauled to the top and set up perpendicularly on a central spot at the summit of the iceberg, the pointed end downward, and a bomb of great power fastened to its upper end. This bomb was one designed to exert its whole explosive power in one direction, and it was so placed that this force would be exerted downward. When all was ready, the electric-wire attachment to the bomb was carried down the iceberg and carefully laid on the ice as the party returned to the Dipsey.

Everybody, of course, was greatly interested in this experiment. The vessel was at least two miles from the iceberg, but in the clear atmosphere the glittering eminence could be plainly seen, and, with a glass, the great iron rod standing high up on its peak was perfectly visible. All were on deck when Mr. Gibbs stood ready to discharge the bomb on top of the rod, and all eyes were fixed upon the iceberg.

There was an explosion—not very loud, even considering the distance—and those who had glasses saw the rod disappear downward. Then a strange grating groan came over the snow-white plain, and the great iceberg was seen to split in half, its two peaks falling apart from each other. The most distant of the two great sections toppled far backward, and with a great crash turned entirely over, its upper part being heavier than its base. It struck an iceberg behind it, slid upon the level ice below, crashed through this, and sank out of sight. Then it was seen to slowly rise again, but this time with its base uppermost. The other and nearest section, much smaller, fell against an adjacent iceberg, where it remained leaning for some minutes, but soon assumed an erect position. The line of cleavage had not been perpendicular, and the greater part of the base of the original iceberg remained upon the nearer section.

When the scene of destruction had been thoroughly surveyed from the deck of the Dipsey, volunteers were called for to go and investigate the condition of affairs near the broken iceberg. Four men, including Mr. Gibbs and Mr. Marcy, went out upon this errand, a dangerous one, for they did not know how far the ice in their direction might have been shattered or weakened by the wreck of the iceberg. They found that little or no damage had been done to the ice between them and the nearer portion of the berg, and, pursing an eastward course on their sledges, they were enabled to look around this lofty mass and see a body of open water in the vicinity of the more distant section almost covered with floating ice. Pressing forward still farther eastward, and going as far south as they dared, they were enabled at last to see that the two portions of the original iceberg were floating at a considerable distance from each other, and that, therefore, there was nothing to prevent the existence of an open passage between them into the lake.

When the party returned with this report work was suspended, but the next day blasting parties went out. The canal was extended to the base of the nearer iceberg, a small boat was rowed around it, and after a careful survey it was found that unless the sections of the iceberg moved together there was plenty of room for the Dipsey to pass between them.

Frank R. Stockton

When the small boat and the sledges had returned to the vessel, and everything was prepared for the start along the canal and into the lake, one of the men came to Captain Hubbell and reported that the Pole Rovinski was absent. For one brief moment a hope arose in the soul of Samuel Block that this man might have fallen overboard and floated under the ice, but he was not allowed to entertain this pleasant thought. Mr. Marcy had seized a glass, and with it was sweeping the icy plain in all directions.

"Hello!" he cried. "Someone come here! Do you see that moving speck off there to the north? I believe that is the scoundrel."

Several glasses were now directed to the spot.

"It is the Pole!" cried Sammy. "He has stolen a sledge and is running away!"

"Where on earth can he be running to?" exclaimed Mr. Gibbs. "The man is insane!"

Mr. Marcy said nothing. His motor sledge, a very fine one, furnished with an unusually large wheel, was still on the deck. He rushed towards it.

"I am going after him!" he shouted. "Let somebody come with me. He's up to mischief! He must not get away!"

"Mischief!" exclaimed Mr. Gibbs. "I don't see what mischief he can do. He can't live out here without shelter; he'll be dead before morning."

"Not he," cried Sammy. "He's a born devil, with a dozen lives! Take a gun with you, Mr. Marcy, and shoot him if you can't catch him!"

Mr. Marcy took no gun; he had no time to stop for that. In a few moments he was on the ice with his sledge, then away he went at full speed towards the distant moving black object.

Two men were soon following Mr. Marcy, but they were a long way behind him, for their sledges did not carry them at the speed with which he was flying over the ice and snow.

It was not long before Rovinski discovered that he was pursued, and, frequently turning his head backward, he saw that the foremost sledge was gaining upon him; but, crouching as low as he could to avoid a rifle-shot, he kept on his way.

But he could not help turning his head every now and then, and at one of these moments his sledge struck a projecting piece of ice and was suddenly overturned. Rovinski rolled out on the hard snow, and the propelling wheel revolved rapidly in the air. The Pole gathered himself up quickly and turned his sledge back into its proper position. He did this in such haste that he forgot that the wheel was still revolving, and therefore was utterly unprepared to see the sledge start away at a great speed, leaving him standing on the snow, totally overwhelmed by astonishment and rage.

Marcy was near enough to view this catastrophe, and he stopped his sledge and burst out laughing. Now that the fellow was secure, Marcy would wait for his companions. When the others had reached him, the three proceeded towards Rovinski, who was standing facing them and waiting. As soon as they came within speaking distance he shouted:

"Stop where you are! I have a pistol, and I will shoot you in turn if you come any nearer. I am a free man! I have a right to go where I please. I have lost my sledge, but I can walk. Go back and tell your masters I have left their service."

Mr. Marcy reflected a moment. He was armed, but it was with a very peculiar weapon, intended for use on shipboard in case of mutinous disturbances. It was a pistol with a short range, carrying an ammonia shell. If he could get near enough to Rovinski, he could settle his business very quickly; but he believed that the pistol carried by the Pole was of the ordinary kind, and dangerous.

Something must be done immediately. It was very cold; they must soon return to the vessel. Suddenly, without a word, Mr. Marcy started his sledge forward at its utmost speed. The Pole gave a loud cry and raised his right hand, in which he held a heavy pistol. For some minutes he had been standing, his glove off, and this pistol clasped in his hand. He was so excited that he had entirely forgotten the intense coldness of the air. He attempted to aim the pistol and to curl his forefinger around the trigger, but his hand and wrist were stiff, his fingers were stiff. His pistol-barrel pointed at an angle downward; he had no power to straighten it or to pull the trigger. Standing thus, his face white with the rage of impotence and his raised hand shaking as if it had been palsied, he was struck full in the face with the shell from Marcy's wide-mouthed pistol. The brittle capsule burst, and in a second, insensible from the fumes of the powerful ammonia it contained, Rovinski fell flat upon the snow.

When the Pole had been taken back to the vessel, and had been confined below, Mr. Gibbs, utterly unable to comprehend the motives of the man in thus rushing off to die alone amid the rigors of the polar regions, went down to talk to him. At first Rovinski refused to make any answers to the questions put to him, but at last, apparently enraged by the imputation that he must be a weak-minded, almost idiotic, man to behave himself in such an imbecile fashion, he suddenly blazed out:

"Imbecile!" he cried. "Weak-minded! If it had not been for

that accursed sledge, I would have shown you what sort of an imbecile I am. I can't get away now, and I will tell you how I would have been an idiot. I would have gone back to the pole, at least to the little house, where, like a fool, you left the end of your cable open to me, open to anybody on board who might be brave enough to take advantage of your imbecility. I had food enough with me to last until I got back to the pole, and I knew of the 'cache' which you left there. Long, long before you ever reached Cape Tariff, and before your master was ready to announce your discoveries to the world, I would have been using your cable. I would have been announcing my discoveries, not in a cipher, but in plain words; not to Sardis, but to the Observatory at St. Petersburg. I would have proclaimed the discovery of the pole, I would have told of your observations and your experiments; for I am a man of science, I know these things. I would have had the honor and the glory. The north pole would have been Rovinski's Pole; that open sea would have been Rovinski's Sea. All you might have said afterwards would have amounted to nothing; it would have been an old story; I would have announced it long before. The glory would have been mine—mine for all ages to come."

"But, you foolish man," exclaimed Mr. Gibbs, "you would have perished up there—no fire, no shelter but that cabin, and very little food. Even if, kept warm and alive by your excitement and ambition, you had been able to send one message, you would have perished soon afterwards."

"What of that?" said Rovinski. "I would have sent my message; I would have told how the north pole was found. The glory and the honor would have been mine."

When Mr. Gibbs related what was said at this interview, Sammy remarked that it was a great pity to interfere with ambition like that, and Sarah acknowledged to her husband, but to him only, that she had never felt her heart sink as it had sunk when she saw Mr. Marcy coming back with that black-faced and black-hearted Pole with him.

"I felt sure," said she, "that we had got rid of him, and that after this we would not be a party of thirteen. It does seem to me as if it is wicked to take such a creature back to civilized people. It's like carrying diseases about in your clothes, as people used to do in olden times."

"Well," said Sammy, "if we could fumigate this vessel and feel sure that only the bad germs would shrivel, I'd be in favor of doin' it."

In less than two hours after the return of Mr. Marcy with his prisoner, the Dipsey started along the recently made canal, carefully rounded the nearer portion of the broken iceberg, and slowly sailed between the two upright sections. These were sufficiently far apart to afford a perfectly safe passage, but the hearts of those who gazed up on their shining, precipitous sides were filled with a chilling horror, for if a wind had suddenly sprung up, these two great sections of the icy mountain might have come together, cracking the Dipsey as if it had been a nut.

But no wind sprang up; the icebergs remained as motionless as if they had been anchored, and the Dipsey entered safely the harboring waters of Lake Shiver.

CHAPTER XX

"THAT IS HOW I LOVE YOU"

For several days the subject of the great perforation made by the automatic shell was not mentioned between Margaret and Roland. This troubled her a great deal, for she thoroughly understood her lover's mind, and she knew that he had something important to say to her, but was waiting until he had fully elaborated his intended statement. She said nothing about it, because it was impossible for her to do so. It made her feel sick even to think of it, and yet she was thinking of it all the time.

At last he came to her one morning, his face pale and serious. She knew the moment her eyes fell upon him that he had come to tell her something, and what it was he had to tell.

"Margaret," said he, beginning to speak as soon as he had seated himself, "I have made up my mind about that shaft. It would be absolutely wicked if I were not to go down to the bottom and see what is there. I have discovered something— something wonderful —and I do not know what it is. I can form no ideas about it, there is nothing on which I can base any theory. I have done my best to solve this problem without going down, but my telescope reveals nothing, my camera shows me nothing at all."

She sat perfectly quiet, pallid and listening.

"I have thought over this thing by day and by night," he continued, "but the conclusion forces itself upon me, steadily and irresistibly, that it is my duty to descend that shaft. I have carefully considered everything, positively everything, connected with the safety of such a descent. The air in the cavity where my shell now rests is perfectly good; I have tested it. The temperature is simply warm, and there is no danger of quicksands or anything of that sort, for my shell still rests as immovable as when I first saw it below the bottom of the shaft.

"As to the distance I should have to descend, when you come to consider it, it is nothing. What is fourteen miles in a tunnel through a mountain? Some of those on the Great Straightcut Pacific Railroad are forty miles in length, and trains run backward and forward every day without any one considering the danger; and yet there is really more danger from one of those tunnels caving in than in my perpendicular shaft, where caving in is almost impossible.

"As to the danger which attends so great a descent, I have thoroughly provided against that. In fact, I do not see, if I carry out my plans, how there could be any danger, more than constantly surrounds us, no matter what we are doing. In the first place, we should not think of that great depth. If a man fell down any one of the deep shafts in our silver mines, he would be as thoroughly deprived of life as if he should fall down my shaft. But to fall down mine—and I want you to consider this, Margaret, and thoroughly understand it—would be almost impossible. I have planned out all the machinery and appliances which would be necessary, and I want to describe them to you, and then, I am sure, you will see for yourself that the element of danger is more fully eliminated than if I should row you on the lake in a little boat."

She sat quiet, still pale, still listening, her eyes fixed upon him.

"I have devised a car," he said, "in which I can sit comfortably and smoke my cigar while I make the descent. This, at the easy and steady rate at which my engines would move, would occupy less than three hours. I could go a good deal faster if I wanted to, but this would be fast enough. Think of that—fourteen miles in three hours! It would be considered very slow and easy travelling on the surface of the earth. This car would be suspended by a double chain of the very best toughened steel, which would be strong enough to hold ten cars the weight of mine. The windlass would be moved by an electric engine of sufficient power to do twenty times the work I should require of it, but in order to make everything what might be called super-safe, there would be attached to the car another double chain, similar to the first, and this would be wound upon another windlass and worked by another engine, as powerful as the first one. Thus, even if one of these double chains should break—an accident almost impossible—or if anything should happen to one of these engines, there would be another engine more than sufficient for the work. The top of this car would be conical, ending in a sharp point, and made of steel, so that if any fragment in the wall of the tunnel should become dislodged and fall, it would glance from this roof and fall between the side of the car and the inner surface of the shaft; for the car is to be only twenty-six inches in diameter-quite wide enough for my purpose—and this would leave at least ten inches of space all around the car. But, as I have said before, the sides of this tunnel are hard and smooth. The substances of which they are composed have been pressed together by a tremendous force. It is as unlikely that anything should fall from them as that particles should drop from the inside of a rifle-barrel.

"I admit, Margaret, that this proposed journey into the depths of the earth is a very peculiar one, but, after all, it is comparatively an easy and safe performance when compared to other things that men have done. The mountain-climbers of our fathers' time, who used to ascend the highest peaks with nothing but spiked shoes and sharpened poles, ran far more danger than would be met by one who would descend such a shaft as mine.

"And then, Margaret, think of what our friends on board the Dipsey have been and are doing! Think of the hundreds of miles they have travelled through the unknown depths of the sea! Their expedition was fifty times as hazardous as the trip of a few hours which I propose."

Now Margaret spoke.

"But I am not engaged to be married to Samuel Block, or to Mr. Gibbs, or to any of the rest of them."

He drew his chair closer to her, and he took both of her hands in his own. He held them as if they had been two lifeless things.

"Margaret," he said, "you know I love you, and—"

"Yes," she interrupted, "but I know that you love science more."

"Not at all," said he, "and I am going to show you how greatly mistaken you are. Tell me not to go down that shaft, tell me to live on without ever knowing what it is I have discovered, tell me to explode bombs in that great hole until I have blocked it up, and I will obey you. That is how I love you, Margaret."

She gazed into his eyes, and her hands, from merely lifeless things, became infused with a gentle warmth; they moved as if they might return the clasp in which they were held. But she did not speak, she simply looked at him, and he patiently waited. Suddenly she rose to her feet, withdrawing her hands from his hold as if he had hurt her.

"Roland," she exclaimed, "you think you know all that is in my heart, but you do not. You know it is filled with dread, with horror, with a sickening fear, but it holds more than that. It holds a love for you which is stronger than any fear or horror or dread. Roland, you must go down that shaft, you must know the great discovery you have made—even if you should never be able to come back to earth again, you must die knowing what it is. That is how I love you!"

Roland quickly made a step forward, but she moved back as if she were about to seat herself again, but suddenly her knees bent beneath her, and, before he could touch her, she had fallen over on her side and lay senseless on the floor.

CHAPTER XXI

THE CAVE OF LIGHT

Margaret was put into the charge of her faithful house-keeper, and Roland did not see her again until the evening. As she met him she began immediately to talk upon some unimportant subject, and there was that in her face which told him that it was her desire that the great thought which filled both their minds should not be the subject of their conversation. She told him she was going to the sea-shore for a short time; she needed a change, and she would go the next day. He understood her perfectly, and they discussed various matters of business connected with the Works. She said nothing about the time of her return, and he did not allude to it.

On the day that Margaret left Sardis, Roland began his preparations for descending the shaft. He had so thoroughly considered the machinery and appliances necessary for the undertaking, and had worked out all his plans in such detail, in his mind and upon paper, that he knew exactly what he wanted to do. His orders for the great length of chain exhausted the stock of several manufactories, and the engines he obtained were even more powerful than he had intended them to be; but these he could procure immediately, and for smaller ones he would have been obliged to wait.

The circular car which was intended to move up and down the shaft, and the peculiar machinery connected with it, with the hoisting apparatus, were all made in his Works. His skilled artisans labored steadily day and night.

It was ten days before he was ready to make his descent. Margaret was still at the sea-shore. They had written to each other frequently, but neither had made mention of the great shaft. Even when he was ready to go down he said nothing to any one of any immediate intention of descending. There was a massive door which covered the mouth of the pit; this he ordered locked and went away.

The next morning he walked into the building a little earlier than was his custom, called for the engineers, and for Mr. Bryce, who was to take charge of everything connected with the descent, and announced that he was going down as soon as preparations could be made.

Mr. Bryce and the men who were to assist him were very serious. They said nothing that was not necessary. If their employer had been any other man than Roland Clewe it is possible they might have remonstrated with him. But they knew him, and they said and did nothing more than was their duty.

The door of the shaft was removed, the car which had hung high above it was lowered to the mouth of the opening, and Roland stepped within it and seated himself. Above him and around him were placed geological tools and instruments of many kinds; a lantern, food and drink; everything, in fact, which he could possibly be presumed to need upon this extraordinary journey. A telephone was at his side by which he could communicate at any time with the surface of the earth. There were electric bells; there was everything to make his expedition safe and profitable. When he gave the word to start the engines, there were no ceremonies, and nothing was said out of the common.

When the conical top of the car had descended below the surface, a steel grating, with orifices for the passage of the chains, was let down over the mouth of the shaft, and the downward journey was begun. In the floor of the car were grated openings, through which Clewe could look downward; but although the shaft below him was brilliantly illuminated by electric lights placed under the car, it did not frighten him or make him dizzy to look down, for the aperture did not appear to be very far below him. The upper part of the car was partially open, and bright lights shone upon the sides of the shaft.

As he slowly descended, he could see the various strata appearing and disappearing in the order in which he knew them. Not far below the surface he passed cavities which he believed held water; but there was no water in them now. He had expected these, and had feared that upon their edges there might be loosened patches of rock or soil, but everything seemed tightly packed and hard. If anything had been loosened it had gone down already.

Down, down he went until he came to the eternal rocks, where the inside of the shaft was polished as if it had been made of glass. It became warmer and warmer, but he knew that the heat would soon decrease. The character of the rocks changed, and he studied them as he went down, and continually made notes.

After a time the polished rocky sides of the shaft grew to be of a solemn sameness. Clewe ceased to take notes; he lighted a cigar and smoked. He tried to quietly imagine what he would come to when he got to the bottom; it would be some sort of a cave into which his shell had made an opening. He wondered what sort of a cave it would be, and how high the roof of it was from the bottom. He wondered if his gardener had remembered what he had told him about the flower-beds in front of his house; he wanted certain changes made which Margaret had suggested. He tried to keep his mind on the flower-beds, but it drifted away to the cave below. He began to wonder if he would come to some underground body of water where he would be drowned; but he knew that was a silly thought. If the shaft had gone through subterranean reservoirs, the water of these would have run out, and before they reached the bottom of the shaft would have dissipated into mist.

Down, down he went. He looked at his watch; he had been in that car only an hour and a half. Was that possible? He had supposed he was almost at the bottom. Suddenly he thought of the people above, and of the telephone. Why had not some of them spoken to him? It was shameful! He instantly called Bryce, and his heart leaped with joy when he heard the familiar voice in his ear. Now he talked steadily on for more than an hour. He had his gardener called, and he told him all that he wanted done in the flower-beds. He gave many directions in regard to the various operations of the Works. Things had been put back a great deal of late. He hoped soon to have everything going on in the ordinary way. There were two or three inventions in which he took particular interest, and of these he talked at great length with Mr. Bryce. Suddenly, in the midst of some talk about hollow steel rods, he told Bryce to let the engines move faster; there was no reason why the car should go so slowly.

The windlasses moved with a little more rapidity, and Clewe now turned and looked at an indicator which was placed on the side of the car, a little over his head. This instrument showed the depth to which he had descended, but he had not looked at it before, for if there should be anything which would make him nervous it would be the continual consideration of the depth to which he had descended.

Frank R. Stockton

The indicator showed that he had gone down fourteen and one eighth miles. Clewe turned and sat stiffly in his seat. He glanced down and saw beneath him only an illuminated hole, fading away at the bottom. Then he turned to speak to Bryce, but to his surprise he could think of nothing to say. After that he lighted another cigar and sat quietly.

Some minutes passed—he did not know how many—and he looked down through the gratings at the floor of the car. The electric light streamed downward through a deep orifice, which did not fade away and end in nothing; it ended in something dark and glittering. Then, as he came nearer and nearer to this glittering thing, he saw that it was his automatic shell, lying on its side, but he could see only a part of it through the opening of the bottom of the shaft which he was descending. In an instant, as it seemed to him, the car emerged from the narrow shaft, and he seemed to be hanging in the air-at least there was nothing he could see except that great shell, lying some forty feet below him. But it was impossible that the shell should be lying on the air! He rang to stop the car.

"Anything the matter?" cried Bryce, almost at the same instant.

"Nothing at all," Clewe replied. "It's all right, I am near the bottom."

In a state of the highest nervous excitement, Clewe gazed about him. He was no longer in a shaft; but where was he? Look out on what side he would, he saw nothing but the light going out from his lamps, but which seemed to extend indefinitely all about him. There seemed to be no limit to his vision in any direction. Then he leaned over the side of his car and looked downward. There was the great shell directly under him, but under it and around it, extending as far beneath it as it extended in every other direction, was the light from his own lamps, and yet that great shell, weighing many tons, lay as if it rested upon the solid ground!

After a few moments Clewe shut his eyes; they pained him. Something seemed to be coming into them like a fine frost in a winter wind. Then he called to Bryce to let the car descend very slowly. It went down, down, gradually approaching the great shell. When the bottom of the car was within two feet of it, Clewe rang to stop. He looked down at the complicated machine he had worked upon so long, with something like a feeling of affection. This he knew, it was his own. Looking upon its familiar form, he felt that he had a companion in this region of unreality.

Pushing back the sliding door of the car, Clewe sat upon the bottom and cautiously put out his feet and legs, lowering them until they touched the shell. It was firm and solid. Although he knew it must be so, the immovability of the great mass of iron gave him a sudden shock of mysterious fear. How could it be immovable when there was nothing under it?

But he must get out of that car, he must explore, he must find out. There certainly could be no danger so long as he could cling to his shell.

He now cautiously got out of the car and let himself down upon the shell. It was not a pleasant surface to stand upon, being uneven, with great spiral ribs, and Clewe sat down upon it, clinging to it with his hands. Then he leaned over to one side and looked beneath him. The shadows of that shell went down, down, down, until it made him sick to look at it. He drew back quickly, clutched the shell with his arms, and shut his eyes. He felt as if he were about to drop with it into a measureless depth of atmosphere.

But he soon raised himself. He had not come down here to

Frank R. Stockton

be frightened, to let his nerves run away with him. He had come to find out things. What was it that this shell rested upon? Seizing two of the ribs with a strong clutch, he let himself hang over the sides of the shell until his feet were level with its lower side. They touched something hard. He pressed them downward; it was very hard. He raised himself and stood upon the substance which supported the shell. It was as solid as any rock. He looked down and saw his shadow stretching far beneath him. It seemed as if he were standing upon petrified air. He put out one foot and he moved a little, still holding on to the shell. He walked, as if upon solid air, to the foremost end of the long projectile. It relieved him to turn his thoughts from what was around him to this familiar object. He found its conical end shattered and broken.

After a little he slowly made his way back to the other end of the shell, and now his eyes became somewhat accustomed to the great radiance about him. He thought he could perceive here and there faint indications of long, nearly horizontal lines—lines of different shades of light. Above him, as if it hung in the air, was the round, dark hole through which he had descended.

He rose, took his hands from the shell, and made a few steps. He trod upon a horizontal surface, but in putting one foot forward, he felt a slight incline. It seemed to him that he was about to slip downward! Instantly he retreated to the shell and clutched it in a sudden frenzy of fear.

Standing thus, with his eyes still wandering, he heard the bell of the telephone ring. Without hesitation he mounted the shell and got into the car. Bryce was calling him.

"Come up," he said. "You have been down there long enough. No matter what you have found, it is time for you to come up."

Roland Clewe was not accustomed to receive commands, but he instantly closed the sliding door of the car, seated himself, and put his mouth to the telephone.

"All right," he said. "You can haul me up, but go very slowly at first."

The car rose. When it reached the orifice in the top of the cave of light, Clewe heard the conical steel top grate slightly as it touched its edge, for it was still swinging a little from the motion given to it by his entrance; but it soon hung perfectly vertical and went silently up the shaft.

CHAPTER XXII

CLEWE'S THEORY

Seated in the car, which was steadily ascending the great shaft, Roland Clewe took no notice of anything about him. He did not look at the brilliantly lighted interior of the shaft, he paid no attention to his instruments, he did not consult his watch, nor glance at the dial which indicated the distance he had travelled. Several times the telephone bell rang, and Bryce inquired how he was getting along; but these questions he answered as briefly as possible, and sat looking down at his knees and seeing nothing.

When he was half-way up, he suddenly became conscious that he was very hungry. He hurriedly ate some sandwiches and drank some water, and then, again, he gave himself up entirely to mental labor. When, at last, the noise of machinery above him and the sound of voices aroused him from his abstraction, the car emerged upon the surface of the earth, Clewe hastily slid back the door and stepped out. At that instant he felt himself encircled by a pair of arms. Bryce was near by, and there were other men by the engines, but the owner of those arms thought nothing of this.

"Margaret!" cried Clewe, "how came you here?"

"I have been here all the time," she exclaimed; "or, at least, nearly all the time." And as she spoke she drew back and looked at him, her eyes full of happy tears. "Mr. Bryce telegraphed to me the instant he knew you were going down, and I was here before you had descended half-way."

"What!" he cried. "And all those messages came from you?"

"Nearly all," she answered. "But tell me, Roland—tell me; have you been successful? What have you discovered?"

"I am successful," he answered. "I have discovered everything!"

Mr. Bryce came forward.

"I will speak to you all very soon," said Clewe. "I can't tell you anything now. Margaret, let us go. I shall want to talk to you directly, but not until I have been to my office. I will meet you at your house in a very few minutes." And with that he left the building and fairly ran to his office.

A quarter of an hour later Roland entered Margaret's library, where she sat awaiting him. He carefully closed the doors and windows. They sat side by side upon the sofa.

"Now, Roland," she said, "I cannot wait one second longer. What is it that you have discovered?"

"Margaret," said he, "I am afraid you will have to wait a good many seconds. If I were to tell you directly what I have discovered, you would not understand it. I am the possessor of wonderful facts, but I believe also that I am the master of a theory more wonderful. The facts I found out when I got to the bottom of the shaft, but the theory I worked out coming up."

"But give them to me quickly!" she cried. "The facts first—I can wait for the theory."

"No," he said, "I cannot do it; I must tell you the whole thing as I have it, arranged in my mind. Now, in the first place, you must understand that this earth was once a comet."

"Oh, bother your astronomy, I really can't understand it! What did you find in the bottom of that hole?"

"You must listen to me," he said. "You cannot comprehend a thing I say if I do not give it to you in the proper order. There have been a great many theories about comets, but there is only one of them in which I have placed any belief. You know that as a comet passes around the sun, its tail is always pointed away from the sun, so that no matter how rapidly the head shall be moving in its orbit, the end of the tail—in order to keep its position—must move with a rapidity impossible to conceive. If this tail were composed of nebulous mist, or anything of that sort, it could not keep its position. There is only one theory which could account for this position, and that is that the head of a comet is a lens and the tail is light. The light of the sun passes through the lens and streams out into space, forming the tail, which does not follow the comet in the inconceivable manner generally supposed, but is constantly renewed, always, of course; stretching away from the sun!"

"Oh, dear!" ejaculated Margaret. "I have read that."

"A little patience," he said. "When I arrived at the bottom of the shaft, I found myself in a cleft, I know not how large, made in a vast mass of transparent substance, hard as the hardest rock and transparent as air in the light of my electric lamps. My shell rested securely upon this substance. I walked upon it. It seemed as if I could see miles below me. In my opinion, Margaret, that substance was once the head of a comet."

"What is the substance?" she asked, hastily.

"It is a mass of solid diamond!"

Margaret screamed. She could not say one word.

"Yes," said he, "I believe the whole central portion of the earth is one great diamond. When it was moving about in its orbit as a comet, the light of the sun streamed through this diamond and spread an enormous tail out into space; after a time this nucleus began to burn."

"Burn!" exclaimed Margaret.

"Yes, the diamond is almost pure carbon; why should it not burn? It burned and burned and burned. Ashes formed upon it and encircled it; still it burned, and when it was entirely covered with its ashes it ceased to be transparent, it ceased to be a comet; it became a planet, and revolved in a different orbit. Still it burned within its covering of ashes, and these gradually changed to rock, to metal, to everything that forms the crust of the earth."

She gazed upon him, entranced.

"Some parts of this great central mass of carbon burn more fiercely than other parts. Some parts do not burn at all. In volcanic regions the fires rage; where my great shell went down it does not burn at all. Now you have my theory. It is crude and rough, for I have tried to give it to you in as few words as possible."

"Oh, Roland," she cried, "it is absurd! Diamond! Why, people will think you are crazy. You must not say such a thing as that to anybody. It is simply impossible that the greater part of this earth should be an enormous diamond."

Frank R. Stockton

"Margaret," he answered, "nothing is impossible. The central portion of this earth is composed of something; it might just as well be diamond as anything else. In fact, if you consider the matter, it is more likely to be, because diamond is a very original substance. As I have said, it is almost pure carbon. I do not intend to say one word of what I have told you to any one —at least, until the matter has been well considered— but I am not afraid of being thought crazy. Margaret, will you look at these?"

He took from his pocket some shining substances resembling glass. Some of them were flat, some round; the largest was as big as a lemon, others were smaller fragments of various sizes.

"These are pieces of the great diamond which were broken when the shell struck the bottom of the cave in which I found it. I picked them up as I felt my way around this shell, when walking upon what seemed to me like solid air. I thrust them into my pocket, and I would not come to you, Margaret, with this story, until I had gone to my office to find out if these fragments were really diamond. I tested them; their substance is diamond!"

Half dazed, she took the largest piece in her hand.

"Roland," she whispered, "if this is really a diamond, there is nothing like it known to man!"

"Nothing, indeed," said he.

She sat staring at the great piece of glowing mineral which lay in her hand. Its surface was irregular; it had many faces; the subdued light from the window gave it the appearance of animated water. He felt it necessary to speak.

"Even these little pieces," he said, "are most valuable jewels."

She still sat silent, looking at the glowing object she held.

"You see, these are not like the stones which are found in our diamond-fields," he said. "Those, most likely, were little, unconsumed bits of the original mass, afterwards gradually forced up from the interior in the same way that many metals and minerals are forced up, and then rounded and dulled by countless ages of grinding and abrasion, due to the action of rocks or water."

"Roland," she cried, excitedly, "this is riches beyond imagination! What is common wealth to what you have discovered? Every living being on earth could—"

"Ah, Margaret," he interrupted, "do not let your thoughts run that way. If my discovery should be put to the use of which you are thinking, it would bring poverty, not wealth, to the world, and not a diamond on earth would be worth more than a common pebble. Everywhere, in civilized countries and in barbaric palaces, people would see their riches vanish before them as if it had been blighted by the touch of an evil magician."

She trembled. "And these—are they to be valued as common pebbles?"

"Oh no," said he; "so long as that great shaft is mine, these broken fragments are to us riches far ahead of our wildest imaginations."

"Roland," she cried, "are you going down into that shaft for more of them?"

"Never, never, never again," he said. "What we have here is enough for us, and if I were offered all the good that there is in this world, which money cannot buy, I would never go down into that cleft again. There was one moment when I stood in that cave in which an awful terror shot into my soul which I shall never be able to forget. In the light of my electric lamps, sent through a vast transparent mass, I could see nothing, but I could feel. I put out my foot and I found it was upon a sloping surface. In another instant I might have slid—where? I cannot bear to think of it!"

She threw her arms around him and held him tightly.

CHAPTER XXIII

THE LAST DIVE OF THE DIPSEY

When the engines of the Dipsey had stopped, and she was quietly floating upon the smooth surface of Lake Shiver, Mr. Gibbs greatly desired to make a connection with the telegraphic cable which was stretched at the bottom of the ocean, beneath him, and to thus communicate with Sardis, But when this matter was discussed in council, several objections were brought against it, the principal one being that the cable could not be connected with the Dipsey without destroying its connection with the little station near the pole; and although this means of telegraphic communication with regions which might never be visited again might well be considered as possessing no particular value, still it was such a wonderful thing to lay a telegraph line to the pole that it seemed the greatest pity in the world to afterwards destroy it.

The friends of this exploring party had not heard from it since it left the polar sea, but there could be no harm in making them wait a little longer. If the return voyage under the ice should be as successfully accomplished as the first submarine cruise, it would not be very many days before the Dipsey should arrive at Cape Tariff. She would not proceed so slowly as she did when coming north, for now her officers would feel that in a measure they knew the course, and moreover they would not be delayed by the work of laying a cable as they progressed.

So it was agreed that it would be a waste of time and labor to stop here and make connection with the cable, and preparations were made for a descent to a safe depth beneath the surface, when they would start southward on their homeward voyage. Mrs. Sarah Block, wrapped from head to foot in furs, remained on deck as long as her husband would allow her to do so. For some time before her eyes had been slowly wandering around the edge of that lonely piece of water, and it was with an unsatisfied air that she now stood gazing from side to side. At last Sammy took her by the arm and told her she must go below, for they were going to close up the hatchways.

"Well," said Sarah, with a sigh, "I suppose I must give 'em up; they were the warmest and most comfortable ones I had, and I could have thawed 'em out and dried 'em so that they would have been as good as ever. I would not mind leavin' 'em if there was a human bein' in this neighborhood that would wear 'em; but there ain't, and it ain't likely there ever will be, and if they are frozen stiff in the ice somewhere, they may stay here, as good as new, for countless ages!"

Of course everybody was very happy, now that they were returning homeward from a voyage successful beyond parallel in history, and even Rovinski was beginning to assume an air of gratified anticipation. He had been released from his confinement and allowed to attend to his duties, but the trust which had been placed in him when this kindness had been extended to him on a previous occasion was wanting now. Everybody knew that he was an unprincipled man, and that if he could gain access to the telegraph instrument at Cape Tariff he would make trouble for the real discoverer of the north pole; so it was agreed among the officers of the vessel that the strictest watch must be kept on him and no shore privileges be allowed him.

The southward voyage of the Dipsey was an easy one and without notable incident; and at last a lookout who had been posted at the upper skylight reported light from above. This meant that they had reached open water southward of the frozen regions they had been exploring, and the great submarine voyage, the most peculiar ever made by man, was ended. Captain Jim Hubbell immediately put on a heavy pea-jacket with silver buttons, for as soon as the vessel should sail upon the surface of the sea he would be in command.

When the dripping Dipsey rose from the waters of the arctic regions, it might have been supposed that the people on board of her were emerging into a part of the world where they felt perfectly at home. Cape Tariff, to which they were bound, was a hundred miles away, and was itself a lonely spot, often inaccessible in severe weather, and they must make a long and hazardous voyage from it before they could reach their homes; but by comparison with the absolutely desolate and mysterious region they had left, any part of the world where there was a possibility of meeting with other human beings seemed familiar and homelike.

But when the Dipsey was again upon the surface of the ocean, when the light of day was shining unobstructed upon the bold form of Captain Hubbell as he strode upon the upper deck—being careful not to stand still lest his shoes should freeze fast to the planks beneath him—the party on board were not so-well satisfied as they expected to be. There was a great wind blowing, and the waves were rolling high. Not far away, on their starboard bow, a small iceberg, tossing like a disabled ship, was surging towards them, impelled by a biting blast from the east, and the sea was so high that sometimes the spray swept over the deck of the vessel, making it impossible for Captain Hubbell and the others with him to keep dry.

Frank R. Stockton

Still the captain kept his post and roared out his orders, still the Dipsey pressed forward against wind and wave. Her engines were strong, her electric gills were folded close to her sides, and she seemed to feel herself able to contend against the storm, and in this point she was heartily seconded by her captain.

But the other people on board soon began to have ideas of a different kind. It seemed to all of them, including the officers, that this vessel, not built to encounter very heavy weather, was in danger, and even if she should be able to successfully ride out the storm, their situation must continue to be a very unpleasant one. The Dipsey pitched and tossed and rolled and shook herself, and it was the general opinion, below decks, that the best thing for her to do would be to sink into the quiet depths below the surface, where she was perfectly at home, and proceed on her voyage to Cape Tariff in the submarine fashion to which she was accustomed.

It was some time before Captain Hubbell would consent to listen to such a proposition as this, but when a wave, carrying on its crest a lump of ice about the size of a flour barrel, threw its burden on the deck of the vessel, raking it from stem to stern, the captain, who had barely been missed by the grating missile, agreed that in a vessel with such a low rail and of such defective naval principles, it would be better perhaps to sail under the water than on top of it, and so he went below, took off his pea-jacket with the silver buttons, and retired into private life. The Dipsey then sank to a quiet depth and continued her course under water, to the great satisfaction of everybody on board.

On a fine, frosty morning, with a strong wind blowing, although the storm had subsided, the few inhabitants of the little settlement at Cape Tariff saw in the distance a flag floating over the water. The Dipsey had risen to the surface some twenty miles from the Cape and now came bravely on,

Captain Hubbell on deck, his silver buttons shining in the sun. The sea was rough, but everybody was willing to bear with a little discomfort in order to be able to see the point of land which was the end of the voyage on the Dipsey, to let their eyes rest as early as possible upon a wreath of smoke arising from the habitation of human beings, and to catch sight of those human beings themselves.

As soon as the Dipscy arrived in the harbor, Sammy and most of the officers went on shore to open communication with Sardis. Sarah Block stayed on the vessel. She had been on shore when she had arrived at Cape Tariff in the Go Lightly, and her disgust with the methods of living in that part of the world had been freely expressed. So long as she had perfectly comfortable quarters on board the good ship she did not wish to visit the low huts and extremely close quarters in which dwelt the people of the little colony. Rovinski also remained on board, but not because he wanted to do so. A watch was kept upon him; but as the Dipsey was anchored some distance from the landing-place, Mr. Marcy was of the opinion that if he attempted to swim ashore it might be well to let him do so, for if he should not be benumbed in the water into which he would plunge he would certainly be frozen to death as soon as he reached the shore.

The messages which came from Sardis as soon as news had been received of the safe return of the explorers were full of hearty congratulations and friendly welcome, but they were not very long, and Sammy said to Mr. Gibbs that he thought it likely that this was one of Mr. Clewe's busy times. The latter telegraphed that he would send a vessel for them immediately, and as she was now lying at St. John's they would not have to wait very long.

The fact was that the news of the arrival of the Dipsey at Cape Tariff had come to Sardis a week after Clewe's descent into the shaft, and he was absorbed, body and soul, in his underground discoveries. He was not wanting in sympathy, or even affection, for the people who had been doing his work, and his interest in their welfare and their achievements was as great as it ever had been, but the ideas and thoughts which now occupied his mind were of a character which lessened and overshadowed every other object of consideration. Most of the messages sent to Cape Tariff had come from Margaret Raleigh.

CHAPTER XXIV

ROVINSKI COMES TO THE SURFACE

When Sammy Block and his companion explorers had journeyed from Cape Tariff to Sardis, they found Roland Clewe ready to tender a most grateful welcome, and to give full and most interested attention to the stories of their adventures and to their scientific reports. For a time he was willing to allow his own great discovery to lie fallow in his mind, and to give his whole attention to the wonderful achievement which had been made under his direction.

He had worked out his theory of the formation and present constitution of the earth; had written a full and complete report of what he had seen and done, and was ready, when he thought the proper time had arrived, to announce to the world his theories and his facts. Moreover, he had sent to several jewelers and mineralogists some of the smaller fragments which he had picked up in the cave of light, and these specialists, while reporting the material of the specimens purest diamond, expressed the greatest surprise at their shape and brilliancy. They had evidently not been ground or cut, and yet their sharp points and glittering surfaces reflected light as if they had been in the hands of a diamond-cutter. One of these experts wrote to Clewe asking him if he had been digging diamonds with a machine which broke the gems to pieces.

Frank R. Stockton

So the soul of Roland Clewe was satisfied; it seemed to walk the air as he himself once had trod what seemed to him a solid atmosphere. There was now nothing that his ambition might point out which would induce him to endeavor to climb higher in the field of human achievement than the spot on which he stood. From this great elevation he was perfectly willing to look down and kindly consider the heroic performances of those who had reached the pole, and who had anchored a buoy on the extreme northern point of the earth's axis.

Mr. Gibbs's reports, and those of his assistants, were well worked out, and of the greatest value to the scientific world, and every one who had made that memorable voyage on the Dipscy had stories to tell for which editors in every civilized land would have paid gold beyond all former precedent.

But Roland Clewe did not care to say anything to the world until he could say everything that he wished to say. It had been known that he had sent an expedition into Northern waters, but exactly what he intended to do had not been known, and what he had done had not been communicated even to the telegraph-operators at Cape Tariff. These had received despatches in cipher from points far away to the north, but while they transmitted them to Sardis they had no idea of their signification. When everything should be ready to satisfy the learned world, as well as the popular mind, the great discovery of the pole would be announced.

In the meantime there was a suspicion in the journalistic world that the man of inventions who lived at Sardis, New Jersey, had done something out of the common in the North. A party of people, one of them a woman, had been taken up there and left there, and they had recently been brought back. The general opinion was that Clewe had endeavored to found a settlement at some point north of Cape Tariff, probably for purposes of scientific observation, and that he had failed.

The stories of these people, however, would be interesting, and several reporters made visits to Sardis. But they all saw Sammy, and not one of them considered his communications worth more than a brief paragraph.

In a week Mr. Gibbs would have finished his charts, his meteorological, his geological, and geographical reports, and a clear, succinct account of the expedition, written by Clewe himself from the statements of the party, would be ready for publication; and in the brilliantly lighted sky of discovery which now rested, one edge upon Sardis and the other upon the pole, there was but one single cloud, and this was Rovinski.

The ambitious and unscrupulous Pole had been the source of the greatest trouble and uneasiness since he had left Cape Tariff. While there he had found that he could not possibly get ashore, and so had kept quiet; but when on board the vessel which had been sent to them from St. John's, he had soon begun to talk to the crew, and there seemed to be but one way of preventing him from making known what had been done by the expedition before its promoters were ready for the disclosure, and this was to declare him a maniac, whose utterances were of no value whatever. He was put into close confinement, and it was freely reported that he had gone crazy while in the arctic regions, and that his mind had been filled with all sorts of insane notions regarding that part of the world.

It had been intended to put him in jail on a criminal charge, but this would not prevent him from talking; and so, when he arrived in New Jersey, he was sent to an insane asylum, the officers of which were not surprised to receive him, for, in their opinion, a wilder-looking maniac was not, to be found within the walls of the institution.

Early on the morning of the day before the world was to be

Frank R. Stockton

electrified by the announcement of the discovery of the pole, a man named William Cunningham, employed in the Sardis Works, entered the large building which had been devoted to the manufacture of the automatic shell, but which had not been used of late and had been kept locked. Cunningham was the watchman, and had entered to make his usual morning rounds. He had scarcely closed the door behind him when, looking over towards the engines which still stood by the mouth of the shaft made by the automatic shell, he was amazed to see that the car which had been used by Roland Clewe in his descent was not hanging above them.

Utterly unable to understand this state of affairs, he ran to the mouth of the shaft. He found the great trap-door which had closed it thrown back, and the grating which had been made to cover the orifice after the car had descended in its place. The engines were not moving, and the chain on the windlass of one of them appeared not to have been disturbed, but on the other windlass one of the chains had been unwound. Cunningham was so astonished that he could not believe what he saw. He had been there the night before; everything had been in order, the shaft closed, and the trap-door locked. He leaned over the grating and looked down; he could see nothing but a black hole without any bottom. The man did not look long, for it made him dizzy. He turned and ran out of the house to call Mr. Bryce.

Ivan Rovinski was not perhaps a lunatic, but his unprincipled ambition had made him so disregard the principles of ordinary prudence when such principles stood in his way that it could not be said that he was at all times entirely sane. He understood thoroughly why he had been put in an asylum, and it enraged him to think that by this course his enemies had obtained a great advantage over him. No matter what he might say, it was only necessary to point to the fact that he was in a lunatic asylum, or that he had just come out of one, to make his utterances of no value.

But to remain in confinement did not suit him at all, and, after three days' residence in the institution in which he had been placed, he escaped and made his way to a piece of woods about two miles from Sardis, where, early that year, he had built himself a rude shelter, from which he might go forth at night and study, so far as he should be able, the operations in the Works of Roland Clewe. Having safely reached his retreat, he lost no time in sallying forth to spy out what was going on at Sardis.

He was cunning and wary, and a man of infinite resource. It was not long before he found out that the polar discovery had not been announced, but he also discovered from listening to the conversations of some of the workmen in the village, which he frequently visited in a guise very unlike his ordinary appearance, that something extraordinary had taken place in the Sardis Works, of which he had never heard. A great shaft had been sunk, the people said, by accident; Mr. Clewe had gone down it in a car, and it had taken him nearly three hours to get to the bottom. Nobody yet knew what he had discovered, but it was supposed to be something very wonderful.

The night after Rovinski heard this surprising news he was in the building which had contained the automatic shell. As active as a cat, he had entered by an upper window.

Rovinski spent the night in that building. He had with him a dark lantern, and he made the most thorough examination of the machinery at the mouth of the shaft. He was a man of great mechanical ability and an expert in applied electricity. He understood that machinery, with all its complicated arrangements and appliances, as well as if he had built it himself. In fact, while examining it, he thought of some very valuable improvements which might have been made in it. He knew that it was an apparatus for lowering the car to a great depth, and, climbing into the car, he examined

Frank R. Stockton

everything it contained. Coming down, he noticed the grating, and he knew what it was for. He looked over the engines and calculated the strength of the chains on the windlasses. He took an impression of the lock of the trap-door, and when he went away in the very early hours of the morning he understood the apparatus which was intended to lower the car as well as any person who had managed it. He knew nothing about the shaft under the great door, but this he intended to investigate as thoroughly as he had investigated the machinery.

The next night he entered the building very soon after Cunningham had gone his rounds, and he immediately set to work to prepare for his descent into the shaft. He disconnected one of the engines, for he sneeringly said to himself that the other one was more than sufficient to lower and raise the car. He charged and arranged all the batteries and put in perfect working order the mechanism by which Clewe had established a connection between the car and the engines, using one of the chains as a conductor, so that he could himself check or start the engines if an emergency should render it necessary.

Then Rovinski, bounding around like a wild animal in a cage, took out a key he had brought with him, opened the trap-door, lifted it back, and gazed down. He could see a beautifully cut well, but that was all. But no matter how deep it was, he intended to go down to the bottom of it.

He started the engine and lowered the car to the ground. Then he looked up at a grating which hung above it and determined to make use of this protection. He could not lower it in the ordinary way after he had entered the car, but in fifteen minutes he had arranged a pulley and rope by which, after the car had gone below the surface, he could lower the grating to its place. He got in, started down into the dark hole, stopped the engine, lowered the grating, went down a little farther, and turned on the electric lights.

The descent of Rovinski was a succession of the wildest sensations of amazed delight. Stratum after stratum passed before his astonished eyes, and, when he had gone down low enough, he allowed himself the most extravagant expressions of ecstasy. His progress was not so regular and steady as that of Roland Clewe had been. He found that he had perfect control of the engine and car, and sometimes he went down rapidly, sometimes slowly, and frequently he stopped. As he continued to descend, his amazement at the wonderful depth of the shaft became greater and greater and his mind was totally unable to appreciate the situation. Still he was not frightened, and went on down.

At last Rovinski emerged into the cave of light. There he stopped, the car hanging some twenty or thirty feet above the bottom. He looked out, he saw the shell, he saw the vast expanse of lighted nothingness, he tried to imagine what it was that that mass of iron rested upon. If he had not seen it, he would have thought he had come out into the upper air of some bottomless cavern. But a great iron machine nearly twenty feet long could not rest upon air! He thought he might be dreaming; he sat up and shut his eyes; in a few minutes he would open them and see if he still saw the same incomprehensible things.

The downward passage of Rovinski had occupied a great deal more time than he had calculated for. He had stopped so much, and had been so careful to examine the walls of the shaft, that morning had now arrived in the upper world, and it was at this moment, as he sat with his eyes closed, that William Cunningham looked down into the mouth of the shaft.

Cunningham was an observing man, and that morning he had picked up a pin and stuck it in the lapel of his rough coat, but

Frank R. Stockton

he had done this hastily and carelessly. The pin was of a recently invented kind, being of a light, elastic metal, with its head of steel. As Cunningham leaned forward the pin slipped out of his coat; it fell through one of the openings in the grating, and descended the shaft head downward.

For the first quarter of a mile the pin went swiftly in an absolutely perpendicular line, nearly at the middle of the shaft. For the next three-quarters of a mile it went down like a rifle-ball. For the next five miles it sped on as if it had been a planet revolving in space. Then, for eight miles, this pin, falling perpendicularly through a greater distance than any object on this earth had ever fallen perpendicularly, went downward with a velocity like that of light. Its head struck the top of the car, which was hanging motionless in the cave of light; it did not glance off, for its momentum was so great that it would glance from nothing. It passed through that steel roof; it passed through Rovinski's head, through his heart, down through the car, and into the great shell which lay below.

When Mr. Bryce and several workmen came running back with William Cunningham, they were as much surprised as he had been, and could form no theory to account for the disappearance of the car. It could not have slipped down accidentally and descended by its own weight, for the trap-door was open and the grating was in place. They sent in great haste for Mr. Clewe, and when he arrived he wasted no time in conjectures, but instantly ordered that the engine which was attached to the car should be started and its chain wound up.

So great was the anxiety to get the car to the surface of the earth that the engine which raised it was run at as high a speed as was deemed safe, and in a little more than an hour the car came out of the mouth of the shaft, and in it sat Ivan Rovinski, motionless and dead.

No one who knew Rovinski wondered that he had had the courage to make the descent of the shaft, and those who were acquainted with his great mechanical ability were not surprised that he had been able to manage, by himself, the complicated machinery which would ordinarily require the service of several men; but every one who saw him in the car, or after he had been taken out of it, was amazed that he should be dead. There was no sign of accident, no perceptible wound, no appearance, in fact, of any cause why he should be a tranquil corpse and not an alert and agile devil. Even when a post-mortem examination was made, the doctors were puzzled. A threadlike solution of continuity was discovered in certain parts of his body, but it was lost in others, and the coroner's verdict was that he came to his death from unknown causes while descending a shaft. The general opinion was that in some way or other he had been frightened to death.

This accident, much to Roland Clewe's chagrin, discovered to the public the existence of the great shaft. Whether or not he would announce its existence himself, or whether he would close it up, had not been determined by Clewe; but when he and Margaret had talked over the matter soon after the terrible incident, his mind was made up beyond all possibility of change, and, by means of great bombs, the shaft was shattered and choked up for a depth of half a mile from its mouth. When this work was accomplished, nothing remained but a shallow well, and, when this had been filled up with solid masonry, the place where the shaft had been was as substantial as any solid ground.

Now the great discovery was probably shut out forever from the world, but Clewe was well satisfied. He would never make another shaft, and it was not to be expected that men would plan and successfully construct one which would reach down to the transparent nucleus of the earth. The terrible fate, whatever it was, which had overtaken Rovinski,

Frank R. Stockton

should not, if Clewe could help it, overtake any other human being.

"But my great discovery," said he to Margaret, "that remains as wonderful as the sun, and as safe to look upon; for with my Artesian ray I can bore down to the solid centre of the earth, and into it, and any man can study it with no more danger than if he sat in his armchair at home; and if they doubt what I say about the material of which that solid centre is composed, we can show them the fragments of it which I brought up with me."

CHAPTER XXV

LAURELS

Nothing but a perusal of the newspapers, magazines, and scientific journals of the day could give any idea of the enthusiastic interest which was shown all over the civilized world in Roland Clewe's account of the discovery of the north pole. His paper on the subject, which was the first intimation the public had of the great news, was telegraphed to every part of the world and translated into nearly every written language. Sardis became a Mecca for explorers and scientific people at home and abroad, and honors of every kind were showered by geographical and other learned societies upon Clewe and the brave company who had voyaged under the ice.

Each member of the party who had sailed on the Dipsey became a hero and spent most of those days in according receptions to reporters, scholars, travellers, sportsmen, and as many of the general public as could be accommodated.

Sarah Block received her numerous visitors in the parlor of the house which had been occupied by Mr. Clewe (and which he had vacated in her favor the moment he had heard an intimation that she would like to have it), in a beautiful gown made of the silky fibre from the pods of the American milk-weed, then generally used in the manufacture of the finest fabrics.

Sarah fully appreciated her position as the woman who had visited the pole, a position not only unique at the time, but which she believed would always remain so. In every way she endeavored to make her appearance suitable to her new position. She wore the best clothes that her money could buy, and furnished her new house very handsomely. She discarded her old silver andirons and fender, which required continual cleaning, and which would not have been tolerated by her except that they were made of a metal which was now so cheap as to be used for household utensils, and she put in their place a beautiful set of polished brass, such as people used in her mother's time. Whenever Sarah found any one whom she considered worthy to listen, she gave a very full account of her adventures, never omitting the loss of her warm and comfortable shoes, which misfortune, together with the performances of Rovinski, and all the dangers consequent, and the acquaintance of the tame and lonely whale, she attributed to the fact that there were thirteen people on board.

Sammy's accounts were in a more cheerful key, and his principles were not affected by his success. He never had believed that there was any good in finding the pole, and he did not believe it now. When they got there, it was just like any other part of the ocean, and it required a great deal of arithmetic and navigation to find out where it was, even when they were looking at it; besides, as he had found out to his disgust, even when they had discovered it, it was not the real pole to which the needle of the compass points.

Moreover, if there had been any distinctive mark about it, except the buoy which they had anchored there, and even if it really were the pole to which needles should point, there was no particular good in finding it, unless other people could get there. But in regard to any other expedition reaching the open polar sea under the ice, Sammy had grave doubts. If a whale could not get out of that sea there was every reason why nobody else should try to get into it; the Dipsey's entrance was the barest scratch, and he would not try it again if the north pole were marked out by a solid mountain of gold.

Roland Clewe refused in all personal interviews to receive the laudations offered him as the discoverer of the pole. It was true that the expedition had been planned by him, and all the arrangements and mechanisms which had insured its success were of his invention, but he steadily insisted that Mr. Gibbs and Sammy, as representatives of the party, should be awarded the glory of the great discovery.

The remarkable success of this most remarkable expedition aroused a widespread spirit of arctic exploration. Not only were voyages under the ice discussed and planned, but there was a strong feeling in favor of overland travel by means of the electric-motor sledges; and in England and Norway expeditions were organized for the purpose of reaching the polar sea in this way. It was noticed in most that was written and said upon this subject that one of the strongest inducements for arctic expeditions was the fact that there would be found on the shores of the polar sea a telegraph station, by means of which instantaneous news of success could be transmitted.

The interest of sportsmen, especially of the hunters of big game, was greatly excited by the statement that there was a whale in the polar sea. These great creatures being extinct everywhere else, it would be a unique and crowning glory to capture this last survivor of his race; and there were many museums of natural history which were already discussing contracts with intending polar whalers for the purchase of the skeleton of the last whale.

Frank R. Stockton

During all this time of enthusiasm and excitement, Roland Clewe made no reference, in any public way, to his great discovery, which, in his opinion, far surpassed in importance to the world all possible arctic discoveries. He was busily engaged in increasing the penetrating distance of his Artesian ray, and when the public mind should have sufficiently recovered from the perturbation into which it had been thrown by the discovery of the pole, he intended to lay before it the results of his researches into the depths of the earth.

At last the time arrived when he was ready for the announcement of the great achievement of his life. The machinery for the production of the Artesian ray had been removed to the larger building which had contained the automatic shell, and was set up very near the place where the mouth of the great shaft had been.

The lenses were arranged so that the path of the great ray should run down alongside of the shaft and but a few feet from it. The screen was set up as it had been in the other building, and everything was made ready for the operations of the photic borer.

The address which Roland Clewe now delivered to the company was made as brief and as much to the point as possible. The description of the Artesian ray was listened to with the deepest interest and with a vast amount of unexpressed incredulity. What he subsequently said regarding his automatic shell and its accidental descent through fourteen miles of the earth's crust, excited more interest and more incredulity, not entirely unexpressed. Clewe was well known as a man of science, an inventor, an electrician of rare ability, and a person of serious purpose and strict probity, but it was possible for a man of great attainments and of the highest moral character to become a little twisted in his intellect.

When at last the speaker told of his descent into the shaft; of his passage fourteen miles into the interior of the earth; of his discoveries, on which he based his theory that the centre of our globe is one vast diamond, there was a general laugh from the reporters' quarter, and the men of science began to move uneasily in their seats and to talk to each other. Professor Tippengray, her silver hair brushed smoothly back from her pale countenance, sat looking at the speaker through her gold spectacles, as if the rays from her bright eyes would penetrate into the very recesses of his soul. Not an atom of doubt was in her mind; she never doubted, she believed or she disbelieved. At present she believed; she had come there to do that, and she would wait, and when the proper time had come to disbelieve she would do so.

If there had been any disposition in the audience to considerately leave the man of shattered intellect to the care of his friends, it disappeared when Clewe said that he would now be glad to show to all present the workings of the Artesian ray. Crazy as he might be, they wanted to wait and see what he had done. The workmen who had charge of the machinery were on hand, and in a few moments a circle of light was glowing on the ground within the screen. Clewe now announced that he would take those present, one at a time, inside the enclosure and show them how light could be made to penetrate miles downward into the solid earth and rock.

Professor Tippengray was the first one invited to step within the screen. Clewe stood at the entrance ready to explain or to hand her the necessary telescopes; and as the portion of her body which remained visible was between him and the light, there was nothing to disturb his nerves.

The lenses were so set that they could penetrate almost instantly to the depth which had previously been reached, but Clewe made his ray move downward somewhat slowly; he

198   Frank R. Stockton

did not wish, especially to the first observer, to show everything at once.

As she beheld at her feet a great lighted well, extending downward beyond the reach of her sharp eyes, Professor Tippengray stepped back with a scream which caused nearly everybody in the audience to start to his feet. Clewe expected this. He raised his hand to the company, asking them to keep still; then he handed Professor Tippengray a stick.

"Take this," he said, "and strike that disk of light; you will find it as solid ground as that you stand on." She did so.

"It is solid!" she gasped; "but where is the end of the stick?"

He turned off the light; there was the end of the stick, and there was the little patch of sandy gravel, which he stepped upon, stamping heavily as he did so. He then retired outside the screen. Professor Tippengray turned to the audience.

"It is all right, gentlemen," she said; "there is nothing to be afraid of. I am going on with the investigation."

Down, down, down went the light, and, telescope in hand, she stood close to the shining edge of the apparent shaft.

"Presently," Clewe said, "you will see the end of the shaft which my Artesian ray is making; then you will perceive a vast expanse of lighted nothingness; that is the great cleft in the diamond which I described to you. In this, apparently suspended in light, you will notice the broken conical end of an enormous iron shell, the shell which made the real tunnel down which I descended in the car."

At this she turned around and looked at him. Even into her strong mind the sharp edge of distrust began to insert itself.

"Look!" said he.

She looked through her telescope. There was the cave of light; there was the shattered end of the shell.

The hands which held the telescope began to tremble. Quickly Clewe drew her away.

"Now," said he, "do you believe?"

For a few moments she could not speak, and then she whispered, "I believe that I have seen what you have told me I should see."

Now succeeded a period of intense excitement, such as was perhaps never before known in an assembly of scientific people. One by one, each person was led by Clewe inside the screen and shown the magical shaft of light. Each received the revelation according to his nature. Some were dumfounded and knew not what to think, others suspected all sorts of tricks, especially with the telescopes, but a well-known optician, who by Clewe's request had brought a telescope of his own, quickly disproved all suspicions of this kind. Many could not help doubting what they had seen, but it was impossible for them to formulate their doubts, with that wonderful shaft of light still present to their mental visions.

For more than two hours Roland Clewe exhibited the action of his Artesian ray. Then he called the company to order. He had shown them his shaft of light, and now he would give them some facts in regard to the real shaft made by the automatic shell.

Every man who had been concerned in Mr. Clewe's descent into the shaft, and those who had assisted in the sounding and the photographing, as well as the persons who had been

Frank R. Stockton

present when Rovinski was drawn up from its depths, now came forward and gave his testimony. Clewe then exhibited the photographs he had taken with his suspended camera, and to the geologists present these were revelations of absorbing interest; seeing so much that they understood, it was difficult to doubt what they saw and did not understand.

Now that what Clewe had just told them was substantiated by a number of witnesses, and now that they had heard from these men that a plummet, a camera, and a car had been lowered fourteen miles into the bowels of the earth, they had no reason to suppose that the great shaft had existed only in the imagination of one crazy man, and they could not believe that all these assistants and workmen were lunatics or liars. Still they doubted. Clewe could see that in their faces as they intently listened to him.

"My friends," said he, "I have set before you nearly all the facts connected with my experience in the shaft, but one important fact I have not yet mentioned. I am quite sure that few, if any of you, believe that I descended into the cleft of a great diamond lying beneath what we call the crust of the earth. I will now state that before I left that cavity I picked up some fragments of the material of which it is composed, which were splintered off when my shell fell into it. I will show you one of them."

A man brought a table covered with a blue cloth, and from one of his pockets Clewe drew a small bag. Opening this, he took out a diamond which he had brought up from the cave of light, and placed it on the middle of the table.

"This," he said, "is a fragment of the mass of diamond into which I descended. I have called it 'The Great Stone of Sardis.'"

Nobody spoke, nobody seemed to breathe. The huge

diamond, of the form and size of a large lemon, lay glowing upon the dark cloth, its irregular facets—all of them clean-cut and polished, the results of fracture—absorbed and reflected the light, and a halo of subdued radiance surrounded the great gem like a tender mist.

"I brought away a number of fragments of the diamond," said Clewe, his voice sounding as if he spoke into an empty hall, "and some of them have been tested by two of the gentlemen present. Here are the stones which have been tested." And he laid some small pieces on the cloth. "They are of the same material as the large one. I brought them all from what I believe to be the great central core of the earth."

Everybody pressed forward, they surrounded the table. One of the jewelers reverently took up the great stone; then in his other hand he took one of the smaller fragments, which he instantly recognized from its peculiar shape. He looked from one to the other; presently he said:

"They are the same substances. This is a diamond." And he laid the great stone back upon the cloth.

"Is there any other place on the surface of this earth, or is there any mine," inquired a shrill voice from the company, "where one could get a diamond like that?"

"There is no such place known to mortal man," replied the jeweler.

"Then," said the same shrill voice, which belonged to a professor from Harvard, "I think it is the duty of every one present, whose mind is capable of it, to believe that the centre of this earth, or a part of that centre, is a vast diamond; at the same time I would say that my mind is not capable of such a belief."

The public excitement produced by the announcement of the discovery of the pole was a trifle compared to that resulting from the news of the proceedings of that day. Clewe's address, with full accounts by the reporters, was printed everywhere, and it was not long before the learned world had given itself up to the discussion.

From this controversy Roland Clewe kept himself aloof. He had done all that he wanted to do, he had shown all that he cared to show; now he would let other people investigate his facts and his reasonings and argue about them; he would retire—he had done enough.

Professor Tippengray was one of the most enthusiastic defenders of Clewe's theories, and wrote a great deal on the subject.

"Granted," she said, in one of her articles, "that the carboniferous minerals, of which the diamond is one, are derived from vegetable matter, and that wood and plants must have existed before the diamond, where, may I ask, did the prediamond-forests derive their carbon? In what form did it exist before they came into being?"

In another essay she said:

"Half a century ago it was discovered that a man could talk through a thousand miles of wire, and yet now we doubt that a man can descend through fourteen miles of rock."

As to the Artesian ray itself, there could be no doubt whatever, for when Clewe, in one of his experiments, directed it horizontally through a small mountain and objects could be plainly discerned upon the other side, discussions in regard to the genuineness of the action of the photic borer were useless.

In medicine, as well as surgery, the value of the Artesian ray was speedily admitted by the civilized world. To eliminate everything between the eye of the surgeon and the affected portion of a human organism was like the rising of the sun upon a hitherto benighted region.

In the winter, Margaret Raleigh and Roland Clewe were married. They travelled; they lived and loved in pleasant places; and they returned the next year rich in new ideas and old art trophies. They bought a fine estate, and furnished it and improved it as an artist paints a picture, without a thought of the cost of the colors he puts upon it. They were rich enough to have everything they cared to wish for. Undue toil and troubled thought had been the companions of Roland Clewe for many a year, and their company had been imposed upon him by his poverty; now he would not, nor would his wife, allow that companionship to be imposed upon him by his riches.

The Great Stone of Sardis was sold to a syndicate of kings, each member of which was unwilling that this dominant gem of the world should belong exclusively to any royal family other than his own. When a coronation should occur, each member of the syndicate had a right to the use of the jewel; at other times it remained in the custody of one of the great bankers of the world, who at stated periods allowed the inhabitants of said planet to gaze upon its transcendent brilliancy.

But the Works at Sardis were not given up. Margaret was not jealous of her rival, Science, and if Roland had ceased to be an inventor, a discoverer, a philosopher, simply because he had become a rich and happy husband, he would have ceased to be the Roland she had loved so long.

The discovery of the north pole had given him fame and honor; for, notwithstanding the fact that he had never been there, he was always considered as the man who had given to the world its only knowledge of its most northern point.

But in his heart Roland Clewe placed little value upon this discovery. Before Mr. Gibbs had announced the exact location of the north pole, all the students of geography had known where it was; before the eyes of the party on the Dipsey had rested upon the spot pointed out by Mr. Gibbs, it was well understood that the north pole was either an invisible point on the surface of ice or an invisible point on the surface of water. If no possible good could result from a journey such as the Dipsey had made, no subsequent good of a similar kind could ever be expected; for the next submarine vessel which attempted a northern journey under the ice was as likely to remain under the ice as it was to emerge into the open air; and if any one reached the open sea upon motor sledges, it would be necessary for them to carry boats with them if they desired so much as a sight of that weather-vane which, no matter how the wind blew, always pointed to the south.

It was the Artesian ray which Clewe considered the great achievement of his life, and to this he intended to devote the remainder of his working days. It was his object to penetrate deeper and deeper with this ray into the interior of the earth. He could always provide himself with telescopes which would show him the limit reached by his photic borer, and so long as that limit was a transparent disk, illuminated by his great ray, so long he would believe in the existence of the diamond centre of the earth. But when the penetrating light reached something different, then would come the time for a change in his theories.

Discussion and controversy in regard to the discoveries of the Artesian ray continued, often with great earnestness and heat, in learned circles, and there were frequent demands upon Clewe to demonstrate the truth of his descent of fourteen miles below the surface of the earth by an actual exhibition of the shaft he had made or by the construction of another.

But to such requests Clewe turned a deaf ear. It would be impossible for him to open his old shaft. If in any way he could remove the rocks and soil which now blocked up its upper portion for a distance of half a mile, it would be impossible to reconstruct any portion which had been obstructed. The smooth and polished walls of the shaft, which gave Clewe such assurance of safety from falling fragments, would not exist if the tunnel were opened.

As to a new shaft—that would require a new automatic shell, and this Clewe was not willing to construct. In fact, rather than make a new opening to the cave of light, he would prefer that people should doubt that any such cave existed. The more he thought of his own descent into that great cleft, the more he thought of the horrible danger of sliding down some invisible declivity to awful, unknown regions; the more he thought of the mysterious death of Rovinski, the more firmly did he determine that not by his agency should a human being descend again to those mysterious depths. He would do all that he could to enable men to see into the interior of this earth, but he would do nothing to help any man to get there.

The controversies in regard to their discoveries and theory disturbed Roland and Margaret not a whit; they worked steadily, with energy and zeal, and, above all, they worked without that dreadful cloud which so frequently overhangs the laborer in new fields—the fear that the means of labor will disappear before the object of the work shall come in view.

One morning in the early summer, Roland rushed into the room where Margaret sat.

Frank R. Stockton

"I have made a discovery!" he exclaimed. "Come quickly, I want to show it to you!"

The heart of the young wife sank. During all these happy days the only shadow that ever flitted across her sky was the thought that some novel temptation of science might turn her husband from the great work to which he had dedicated himself. Much that he had purposed to do, he had, at her earnest solicitation, set aside in favor of what she considered the greatest task to which a human being could give his time, his labor, and his thought. It had been long since she had heard her husband speak of a new discovery, and the words chilled her spirit.

"Come," he said, "quickly!" And, taking her by the hand, he led her out upon the lawn.

Over the soft green turf, under the beautiful trees, by the bright flowers of the parterres and through the natural beauty of the charming park, he led her; but not a word did she say of the soft colors and the soft air. Not a flower did she look at. It seemed to her as if she trod a bleak and stony road. She dreaded what she might hear, what she might see.

He led her hastily through a gate in the garden wall; they passed through the garden, and, whispering to her to step lightly, they entered a quiet, shady spot beyond the house grounds.

"This way," he whispered. "Stoop down. Do you see that shining thing with bright-red patches of color? It is an old tomato-can; a robin has built her nest in it; there are three dear little birds inside; the mother-bird is away, and I wanted you to come before she returned. Isn't it lucky that I should have found that? And here, in our own grounds? I don't believe there was ever another robin who made her nest in a tomato-can!"

Doubtless the two birds who had made that nest sincerely loved each other; and there were at that moment a great many other birds, and a great many men and women, in the same plight, but never anywhere did any human being possess a soul so happy as that of Margaret at that moment.

"Roland," she said, "when I first knew you, you would not have noticed such a little thing as that."

"I couldn't afford it," he said.

"It is the sweetest charm of all your triumphs!" said she.

"What is?" he asked.

"That you feel able to afford it now," answered Margaret.

Samuel Block and his wife Sarah found that life grew pleasanter as they grew older. Fortunate winds had blown down to them from the distant north; the substantial rewards of the enterprise were eminently satisfactory, and the honors which came to them were not at all unwelcome even to the somewhat cynical Samuel.

Sitting one evening with his wife before a cheering fire—for both of them were wedded to the old-fashioned ways of keeping warm—Sammy laid down the daily paper with a smile.

"There's an account here," he said, "of a lot o' fools who are goin' to fit out a submarine-ship to try to go under the ice to the pole, as we did. They may get there, and they may get back; they may get there, and they may never get back; and they may never get there, and never get back; but whichever of the three it happens to be, it'll be of no more good than if they measured a mile to see how many inches there was in it."

"Sammy," exclaimed Sarah, "I do think you are old enough to stop talkin' such nonsense as that. To be sure, there was a good many things that I objected to in that voyage to the pole. In the first place, there was thirteen people on board, which was the greatest mistake ever committed by a human explorin' party; and then, agin, there was no provision for keepin' whales from bumpin' the ship, and if you knew the number of hours that I laid awake on that Dipsey thinkin' what would happen if the frolicsome whale determined not to be left alone, and should follow us into narrow quarters, you would understand my feelin's on that subject; but as to sayin' there wasn't no good in the expedition —I think that's downright wickedness. Look at that fender; look at them andirons, them beautiful brass candlesticks, and that shovel and tongs, with handles shinin' like gold! If it hadn't been that we discovered the pole, and so got able to afford good furniture, all those handsome things would have been made of common silver, just as if they was pots and kittles, or garden-spades!"

ABOUT THE AUTHOR

 **Frank R. Stockton** (April 5, 1834 - April 20, 1902), was an American writer and humorist, best known today for a series of innovative children's fairy tales that were widely popular during the last decades of the 19th century. Stockton avoided the didactic moralizing common to children's stories of the time, instead using clever humor to poke at greed, violence, abuse of power and other human foibles, describing his fantastic characters' adventures in a charming, matter-of-fact way in stories like "The Griffin and the Minor Canon" (1885) and "The Bee-Man of Orn" (1887), which was republished in 1964 in an edition illustrated by Maurice Sendak.

Born in Philadelphia, Stockton was the son of a prominent Methodist minister who discouraged him from a writing career. He supported himself as a wood engraver until his father's death in 1860; in 1867, he moved back to Philadelphia to write for a newspaper founded by his brother. His first fairy tale, "Ting-a-ling," was published that year in The Riverside Magazine; his first book collection appeared in 1870.

He died of a cerebral hemorrhage in 1902. His collected works, 23 volumes of stories for adults and children, were published between 1899 and 1904.

Choose from Thousands of 1stWorldLibrary Classics By

A. M. Barnard	Booth Tarkington	Edward Everett Hale
Ada Leverson	Boyd Cable	Edward J. O'Biren
Adolphus William Ward	Bram Stoker	Edward S. Ellis
Aesop	C. Collodi	Edwin L. Arnold
Agatha Christie	C. E. Orr	Eleanor Atkins
Alexander Aaronsohn	C. M. Ingleby	Eleanor Hallowell Abbott
Alexander Kielland	Carolyn Wells	Eliot Gregory
Alexandre Dumas	Catherine Parr Traill	Elizabeth Gaskell
Alfred Gatty	Charles A. Eastman	Elizabeth McCracken
Alfred Ollivant	Charles Amory Beach	Elizabeth Von Arnim
Alice Duer Miller	Charles Dickens	Ellem Key
Alice Turner Curtis	Charles Dudley Warner	Emerson Hough
Alice Dunbar	Charles Farrar Browne	Emilie F. Carlen
Allen Chapman	Charles Ives	Emily Bronte
Alleyne Ireland	Charles Kingsley	Emily Dickinson
Ambrose Bierce	Charles Klein	Enid Bagnold
Amelia E. Barr	Charles Hanson Towne	Enilor Macartney Lane
Amory H. Bradford	Charles Lathrop Pack	Erasmus W. Jones
Andrew Lang	Charles Romyn Dake	Ernie Howard Pie
Andrew McFarland Davis	Charles Whibley	Ethel May Dell
Andy Adams	Charles Willing Beale	Ethel Turner
Angela Brazil	Charlotte M. Braeme	Ethel Watts Mumford
Anna Alice Chapin	Charlotte M. Yonge	Eugene Sue
Anna Sewell	Charlotte Perkins Stetson	Eugenie Foa
Annie Besant	Clair W. Hayes	Eugene Wood
Annie Hamilton Donnell	Clarence Day Jr.	Eustace Hale Ball
Annie Payson Call	Clarence E. Mulford	Evelyn Everett-green
Annie Roe Carr	Clemence Housman	Everard Cotes
Annonaymous	Confucius	F. H. Cheley
Anton Chekhov	Coningsby Dawson	F. J. Cross
Archibald Lee Fletcher	Cornelis DeWitt Wilcox	F. Marion Crawford
Arnold Bennett	Cyril Burleigh	Fannie E. Newberry
Arthur C. Benson	D. H. Lawrence	Federick Austin Ogg
Arthur Conan Doyle	Daniel Defoe	Ferdinand Ossendowski
Arthur M. Winfield	David Garnett	Fergus Hume
Arthur Ransome	Dinah Craik	Florence A. Kilpatrick
Arthur Schnitzler	Don Carlos Janes	Fremont B. Deering
Arthur Train	Donald Keyhoe	Francis Bacon
Atticus	Dorothy Kilner	Francis Darwin
B.H. Baden-Powell	Dougan Clark	Frances Hodgson Burnett
B. M. Bower	Douglas Fairbanks	Frances Parkinson Keyes
B. C. Chatterjee	E. Nesbit	Frank Gee Patchin
Baroness Emmuska Orczy	E. P. Roe	Frank Harris
Baroness Orczy	E. Phillips Oppenheim	Frank Jewett Mather
Basil King	E. S. Brooks	Frank L. Packard
Bayard Taylor	Earl Barnes	Frank V. Webster
Ben Macomber	Edgar Rice Burroughs	Frederic Stewart Isham
Bertha Muzzy Bower	Edith Van Dyne	Frederick Trevor Hill
Bjornstjerne Bjornson	Edith Wharton	Frederick Winslow Taylor

Friedrich Kerst	Hayden Carruth	James Branch Cabell
Friedrich Nietzsche	Helent Hunt Jackson	James DeMille
Fyodor Dostoyevsky	Helen Nicolay	James Joyce
G.A. Henty	Hendrik Conscience	James Lane Allen
G.K. Chesterton	Hendy David Thoreau	James Lane Allen
Gabrielle E. Jackson	Henri Barbusse	James Oliver Curwood
Garrett P. Serviss	Henrik Ibsen	James Oppenheim
Gaston Leroux	Henry Adams	James Otis
George A. Warren	Henry Ford	James R. Driscoll
George Ade	Henry Frost	Jane Abbott
Geroge Bernard Shaw	Henry James	Jane Austen
George Cary Eggleston	Henry Jones Ford	Jane L. Stewart
George Durston	Henry Seton Merriman	Janet Aldridge
George Ebers	Henry W Longfellow	Jens Peter Jacobsen
George Eliot	Herbert A. Giles	Jerome K. Jerome
George Gissing	Herbert Carter	Jessie Graham Flower
George MacDonald	Herbert N. Casson	John Buchan
George Meredith	Herman Hesse	John Burroughs
George Orwell	Hildegard G. Frey	John Cournos
George Sylvester Viereck	Homer	John F. Kennedy
George Tucker	Honore De Balzac	John Gay
George W. Cable	Horace B. Day	John Glasworthy
George Wharton James	Horace Walpole	John Habberton
Gertrude Atherton	Horatio Alger Jr.	John Joy Bell
Gordon Casserly	Howard Pyle	John Kendrick Bangs
Grace E. King	Howard R. Garis	John Milton
Grace Gallatin	Hugh Lofting	John Philip Sousa
Grace Greenwood	Hugh Walpole	John Taintor Foote
Grant Allen	Humphry Ward	Jonas Lauritz Idemil Lie
Guillermo A. Sherwell	Ian Maclaren	Jonathan Swift
Gulielma Zollinger	Inez Haynes Gillmore	Joseph A. Altsheler
Gustav Flaubert	Irving Bacheller	Joseph Carey
H. A. Cody	Isabel Cecilia Williams	Joseph Conrad
H. B. Irving	Isabel Hornibrook	Joseph E. Badger Jr
H.C. Bailey	Israel Abrahams	Joseph Hergesheimer
H. G. Wells	Ivan Turgenev	Joseph Jacobs
H. H. Munro	J.G.Austin	Jules Vernes
H. Irving Hancock	J. Henri Fabre	Julian Hawthrone
H. R. Naylor	J. M. Barrie	Julie A Lippmann
H. Rider Haggard	J. M. Walsh	Justin Huntly McCarthy
H. W. C. Davis	J. Macdonald Oxley	Kakuzo Okakura
Haldeman Julius	J. R. Miller	Karle Wilson Baker
Hall Caine	J. S. Fletcher	Kate Chopin
Hamilton Wright Mabie	J. S. Knowles	Kenneth Grahame
Hans Christian Andersen	J. Storer Clouston	Kenneth McGaffey
Harold Avery	J. W. Duffield	Kate Langley Bosher
Harold McGrath	Jack London	Kate Langley Bosher
Harriet Beecher Stowe	Jacob Abbott	Katherine Cecil Thurston
Harry Castlemon	James Allen	Katherine Stokes
Harry Coghill	James Andrews	L. A. Abbot
Harry Houidini	James Baldwin	L. T. Meade

L. Frank Baum
Latta Griswold
Laura Dent Crane
Laura Lee Hope
Laurence Housman
Lawrence Beasley
Leo Tolstoy
Leonid Andreyev
Lewis Carroll
Lewis Sperry Chafer
Lilian Bell
Lloyd Osbourne
Louis Hughes
Louis Joseph Vance
Louis Tracy
Louisa May Alcott
Lucy Fitch Perkins
Lucy Maud Montgomery
Luther Benson
Lydia Miller Middleton
Lyndon Orr
M. Corvus
M. H. Adams
Margaret E. Sangster
Margret Howth
Margaret Vandercook
Margaret W. Hungerford
Margret Penrose
Maria Edgeworth
Maria Thompson Daviess
Mariano Azuela
Marion Polk Angellotti
Mark Overton
Mark Twain
Mary Austin
Mary Catherine Crowley
Mary Cole
Mary Hastings Bradley
Mary Roberts Rinehart
Mary Rowlandson
M. Wollstonecraft Shelley
Maud Lindsay
Max Beerbohm
Myra Kelly
Nathaniel Hawthrone
Nicolo Machiavelli
O. F. Walton
Oscar Wilde

Owen Johnson
P.G. Wodehouse
Paul and Mabel Thorne
Paul G. Tomlinson
Paul Severing
Percy Brebner
Percy Keese Fitzhugh
Peter B. Kyne
Plato
Quincy Allen
R. Derby Holmes
R. L. Stevenson
R. S. Ball
Rabindranath Tagore
Rahul Alvares
Ralph Bonehill
Ralph Henry Barbour
Ralph Victor
Ralph Waldo Emmerson
Rene Descartes
Ray Cummings
Rex Beach
Rex E. Beach
Richard Harding Davis
Richard Jefferies
Richard Le Gallienne
Robert Barr
Robert Frost
Robert Gordon Anderson
Robert L. Drake
Robert Lansing
Robert Lynd
Robert Michael Ballantyne
Robert W. Chambers
Rosa Nouchette Carey
Rudyard Kipling
Saint Augustine
Samuel B. Allison
Samuel Hopkins Adams
Sarah Bernhardt
Sarah C. Hallowell
Selma Lagerlof
Sherwood Anderson
Sigmund Freud
Standish O'Grady
Stanley Weyman
Stella Benson
Stella M. Francis

Stephen Crane
Stewart Edward White
Stijn Streuvels
Swami Abhedananda
Swami Parmananda
T. S. Ackland
T. S. Arthur
The Princess Der Ling
Thomas A. Janvier
Thomas A Kempis
Thomas Anderton
Thomas Bailey Aldrich
Thomas Bulfinch
Thomas De Quincey
Thomas Dixon
Thomas H. Huxley
Thomas Hardy
Thomas More
Thornton W. Burgess
U. S. Grant
Upton Sinclair
Valentine Williams
Various Authors
Vaughan Kester
Victor Appleton
Victor G. Durham
Victoria Cross
Virginia Woolf
Wadsworth Camp
Walter Camp
Walter Scott
Washington Irving
Wilbur Lawton
Wilkie Collins
Willa Cather
Willard F. Baker
William Dean Howells
William le Queux
W. Makepeace Thackeray
William W. Walter
William Shakespeare
Winston Churchill
Yei Theodora Ozaki
Yogi Ramacharaka
Young E. Allison
Zane Grey